The Age of Cities

# The Age of Cities

# Brett Josef Grubisic

ARSENAL PULP PRESS

Vancouver

ARSENAL PULP PRESS
200 – 341 Water Street
Vancouver, BC
Canada V6B 1B8
*arsenalpulp.com*

The publisher gratefully acknowledges the support of the Canada
Council for the Arts and the British Columbia Arts Council for
its publishing program, the Government of Canada through
the Book Publishing Industry Development Program, and the
Government of British Columbia through the Book Publishing
Tax Credit Program for its publishing activities.

This is a work of fiction. Any resemblance of characters to per-
sons either living or deceased is purely coincidental.

Text design by Shyla Seller
Cover design by Airedale Monthly
Author photograph by Rosamond Norbury
Cover photograph from the Vancouver Public Library, Special
    Collections, VPL 6103. Used with permission.

Printed and bound in Canada on ancient forest friendly paper

**Library and Archives Canada Cataloguing in Publication**

Grubisic, Brett Josef

    The age of cities / Brett Josef Grubisic.

ISBN 1-55152-212-8

    I. Title.

PS8613.R82A63 2006        C813'.6        C2006-902502-9

ISBN13 978-155152-212-8

*for the Marks*
*and their inadvertence*

# Acknowledgements

Writing a novel turned out to be weirder and far less straightforward than I'd expected. To the friends and colleagues who offered words and minutes of encouragement, then, thank you. I'd also like to dedicate especial thanks to Carellin (for telling me that typing would be better than complaining), Michael, George, David, and Matt (for generosity tempered with criticism during and after writing group meetings), Monica (for the kind of praise only the mother of one's ex can utter), Bryan (for being a friend), and Lefler (ditto—and having a keen eye). Thanks as well to the folks at Arsenal for being good sports. Not least: my wholehearted gratitude to Meesha and Shalia for being there.

# THE AGE OF CITIES

*a literary artifact*

edited by A.X. Palios

And yet nothing serves so well to strengthen them
As staving off the darts of heedless love,
No matter stallions or bulls your herd.
For which reason they banish bulls to distant fields,
Cut off by peaks and beyond broad streams,
Or close them in behind doors with mangers full.

—Virgil, *The Georgics* [unpublished translation][1]

And eyeless Nature that makes you drink
From the cup of Love, though you know it's poisoned;
To whom would your flower-face have been lifted?
Botanist, weakling? Cry of what blood to yours?—
Pure or foul, for it makes no matter,
It's blood that calls to our blood.

—Edgar Lee Masters, *Spoon River Anthology*

---

1. For an in-depth discussion of the exceptional bibliographic circumstance
of the forthcoming manuscript, please see Afterword (An Introduction),
pp. 216–240. —*A.X. Palios, editor*

# Prol[ogue] S[eptember 19]58

Mrs. Pierce's Social Studies 11 class shuffled through the library door at 10:15.

Standing on his footstool at the end of the Literature aisle, Winston turned to watch his colleague's watery form through the frosted glass. A blurred left arm held the door open while the other hastened students toward his desk with a polite urgency: she'd told Winston what time they would arrive and she considered her word to be as good as law. Mrs. Pierce passed one last dawdling student through, followed him in, and delivered a shy smile to Winston as he left the stacks.

This juvenile swarm was unprecedented, the result of meetings that had taken place over the past summer. Winston had not attended even one; his interest in the school's rules and regulations ended at the library door. Yesterday in the staff room, the Vice-Principal, Mr. Westburn, had made a formal announcement about the new school policy: that teachers would lead several of their classes on a kind of field trip, one strictly limited to the nooks and crannies of the school. The notion behind it, Mrs. Pierce had explained after the Vice-Principal had turned over the floor to her, was that young spongy brains would be keen to absorb knowledge and direction from this wide exposure to options. Ideally, anyway, that was the hope.

Winston had felt thrown out of orbit by the mass of faces an hour before, but now their sudden arrival and departure seemed no different than the other routines the staff had been following for years. He knew that Mrs. Pierce would expect to hear his opinion on the merits of the tours, and stored away this realization for later use.

Delilah Pierce was a veteran committee member and a tireless promoter of schooling. She fervently believed in the high school's ongoing development (an immaculately stitched aphorism, coined by herself—

A Great Education is an Excellent Resource.
A Great School is an Evolving Organism.

—sat snug within a pewter frame on her desk, presented to her by a thankful graduate semesters before), and Winston had observed that she encountered no difficulty whatsoever in transforming ideas into action. School was fertile ground, she had exclaimed more than once, and she thrived on it. About school he agreed with her in principle, though not in order of magnitude.

Winston had heard about the school tour policy a week before summer vacation ended because Delilah had scheduled time for home visits to help spread the word. The wispy and nervous devotee of Andrew Carnegie had sheltered herself in the backyard shade as Winston lay stretched out in the sunlit lawn chair and his mother puttered about in her tremendous garden. Such standoffishness was practical: Delilah feared cats and kept watch on Grendel—sprawled under the chair, plump as a panda bear—as though his utter languor were a sly pose that hid a lion's savage heart. Delilah had dropped by the house (having telephoned well beforehand, of course, to make certain that she was not imposing on their hospitality) to fill him in on the Curriculum Development Committee's *evolutionary step*. They were practically neighbours, Delilah had chirped, so it was no trouble at all to explain the whole plan in person. And besides, the Committee's scheme would be starting up within days; she'd said with a blush that she had volunteered to talk to all the high school staff living close by. Winston called her Sister Delilah and was fond of teasing her about living too much for the benefit of others.

Winston had listened to her and then wondered aloud if the Committee's plan was in fact *curricular*; shielding his eyes from the sun with a hand shaped into a stiff salute he asked if perhaps she ought to blaze ahead with a Pedagogy Committee. "There can never be too many committees, I'd venture to say," he'd remarked.

"I'll deign not to answer your sarcasm, Mr. Wilson," she'd said with disingenuous ruffled feathers. "You shouldn't scoff." She shook her index finger in mock warning. "Really, if no one lets them know that there are choices, then they won't make any. Ignorance is not bliss, is it? Who knows, a future librarian might have his eureka when his Chemistry class is led into your corner of the building."

"Another great idea, Delilah," Alberta had remarked from her bower of plum tomatoes, pungent now in the late summer heat.

"Thank you, Mrs. Wilson," she'd said, her shifting eyes showing Winston a flash of puzzlement. Winston imagined that the uncertainty resulted from his mother's bland comment. Acquaintances were rarely satisfied that they could accept her words at face value.

Social Studies 11 was the second class to pass through his library this morning. The first had been the plainly cowed Biology 10 class of Miss Mittchel ("That's with double Ts and a single L, please take note," she'd tell her classes each year—an odd medley of prim and proud—only to be mocked for the year, renamed as Miss Dewwlapp: the Biology teacher had once been a corpulent young lady with gland problems, and in places her stretched skin remained loose long after the success of the Reducing Plan she'd share with the other ladies with the slightest encouragement.) For her students Winston had talked about agriculture, forestry, and the local flora and fauna—"Bryophyte, from the Latin words for 'moss' and 'plant,'" "*Pediculus humanus capitus*, the head louse, which we hope not to encounter if we value our hair"—before walking them through the modest miracles of the Dewey Decimal system.

Winston adjusted the smoothly oiled pivot of his desk chair by a few degrees, and jotted down a reminder to bring in a jar of his mother's dilled carrots to the diligent janitor Mr. Horvath. Not just anyone would remember to stop bothersome squeaks; and Winston had merely mentioned it in passing in late June. He turned his attention to the matter now at hand. Wearing her favourite white cardigan over her shoulders this morning, Delilah waded through the crowd toward his desk. When she nodded Winston quickly surveyed the class and began with words he'd prepared en route to school that morning.

"Hello, students. For those who are new to the high school my name is Mr. Wilson. This library is where you're going to find me." He unclasped and spread his hands to emphasize the breadth of the room. Delilah Pierce hoped to offer up a world of promise and possibilities, and he would strive to introduce some of it to them.

The thirty faces were watching him, expectant. Often enough, Miss Mittchel had remarked on his sonorous voice in her efforts to have him join her choir, and he was aware that he could use its lower register to sway or—when he was much younger—intimidate. The technique worked with all manner of animal, he'd discovered over the years. He thumped his chest as he cleared his throat.

"Since class assignments from Mrs. Pierce will undoubtedly have you appearing here for many hours to come"—a low chorus of sighs and groans arose—"your teacher has had the foresight to give you a head start. Today, I will show you how the library can help you obtain an A in your Social Studies class. On all other school days until the end of June, I am here to answer your questions and assist you in getting your scholarly tasks accomplished."

He could see and hear the fidgeting starting. A whiff of brimstone would stifle it.

"Oh, yes, I may have been premature about your A grades. As with many parts of life, success is not as easy as all that. Just as our province's economy relies on raw resources, so too do you. The library offers you such material, though what you make of it is ultimately up to you. As that pertains to a grade, in other words, your endeavours determine your fate. For the most part." Turning to their teacher, he raised his brow.

He surveyed the faces. They were impatient for the library tour to conclude. So much for eager sponges, he thought.

"I will try to illustrate the library's usefulness with an example. Let's say you have been given an assignment that requires you to examine an aspect of your home town. Now, for those of you who have grown up here, River Bend City is as it has long been, a community of farmers and loggers who support our bustling merchants on 1st Avenue. So, then, what essay could you possibly write?"

He hadn't anticipated anyone answering his rhetorical question, but paused for a moment just in case. No one dared a word.

"Well, the official history of River Bend City is a different beast altogether, you see. Its origins, its roots are a complicated entanglement of mercantile schemes and religious devotion."

The promise of intrigue and mystery had grabbed their attention.

"Our thriving town also has two points of origin." He turned his hands palm upward, as though he was Justice come to life and holding out the two possibilities for them to examine up close. "On the one hand, Oblates of Mary Immaculate founded a mission here in 1862—at the time, our local volcano"—and here he angled his face toward the window directly behind his desk—"was still sending up plumes of smoke like an angry Samoan god.

"Now then, one Father Pourguet led these men just east of here, aiming all the while to rescue the Indians from themselves, or, to be more accurate, themselves after gold rush fools and agents of government had trampled them and innocent carriers had spread smallpox to them. Smallpox alone made their population in the area shrink from 30,000 to 6,000—that's a reduction of eighty percent, as any of your mathematically skilled peers could tell you. To give you a clearer picture, that would be similar (if our 1956 census is at all reliable) to the current population of our fair city suddenly dropping to just over 2,000 souls, many of their lives in ruin."

He heard some murmuring and ran his eyes along the group.

"And yet—on the other hand—not too many years later, and a few miles to the southwest, the town's second history began. Presto, just like that. So you may not have heard of it, but our city was the invention, from noon to two p.m. on a mild spring day in 1891 to be precise, of an inspired land speculator, who sold exactly 300 lots—the same thing he'd done a decade earlier, but this time in the Prairies.

"Here. You see. It was advertised as an auction, come one, come all." Winston held up a piece of paper, a facsimile of an actual newspaper advertisement—

**GREAT Auction Sale of**
**300 City Lots**

# RIVER BEND CITY

**on Tuesday May 19**

**Tickets for the Round trip**

From New Westminster and Return, Same Day   75¢

From Vancouver and Return, Same Day   $2.00

He reached across his desk and handed it to Mrs. Pierce. "Please be careful," she whispered when she passed it to a nearby student.

"The man had an auction pavilion—washed away by spring flooding decades ago—built down on the flats, and folks from all over the new province and Washington State came up to buy up a lot or two. For months before, our secular founding father had been promising that this unexceptional stretch of green along the river would soon be an important hub of economic prosperity. Once auctioned off, he'd apparently tell anyone he met, it would grow faster than the Royal City had some years before. A bonanza for the businessman with vision."

"How do I know all this, you might ask." He supposed most of them would never ask such a question. They were restless, he could see, lost in their skittish teenaged thoughts—conjuring pierced hearts, patterns for autumn outfits or souped-up cars in their heads—and looking over his shoulder and through the window into September's washed-out blue sky. "The answer, of course, involves the books and materials that are available right here in the library. Any questions?" He gave his attention to Mrs. Pierce in the ensuing silence.

Instantly hawkish, she surveyed her class. "It would seem that you might have something to say, Miss Schmidt." Everyone turned to look at a willowy black-haired girl standing at the rear of the group. She shook her head and stared at the floor, hands clutching her plaid skirt.

"Mr. Gruber, then? You two appeared to be involved in quite an in-depth conversation, whispered though it was. Perhaps you'd care to share it with us?" Although Mrs. Pierce kept her hands primly folded at her waist she brooked no disruptions.

The youth was solid and swarthy, Winston noticed, and the gleam in his assured green eyes hinted that he could become a trouble student any time soon. Likely born with a hockey stick in his hand.

"Well, Mrs. Pierce," he replied in a baritone steady and insinuating, "we were just wondering about when and why this town became such a backwater. That would be an interesting essay, wouldn't it?" He started to say more, but stalled.

Mrs. Pierce gave him no reply. "Any other questions," she asked. She instructed the class to thank Mr. Wilson for his time.

Winston did not believe the young man's question was rhetorical. He spoke to the Social Studies teacher for a moment before she shepherded her group back to their classroom.

"'To each thing there is a season?'" he said, thinking of the youth's provocation. Each time he stood close to her he marveled at their difference: she was so compact, her body seemed to take up no space.

"As we all know, it is perfectly lovely here." Her face gave him no reason to doubt the sincerity of her affection for the town. "The boy was just showing off for that suddenly bashful Miss Schmidt. If he owned an automobile, he'd be revving the engine. The business of birds and bees never ceases," she continued, tut-tutting with a nun's bride of Christ puzzlement.

"I'd like to hear from you about these tours. See what we can do to improve them. During lunch hour, perhaps?" She hurried to catch up with her class, small quick steps across the buffed linoleum squares.

There was no believing that the sisters at St. Margaret's would not welcome her with open arms—a prodigal daughter—Winston concluded as she directed her students with soft and urgent words of enthusiasm.

He walked home basking in the diffuse warmth of the sun; wispy cirrus fingers pointed high above and coaxed out his pang of regret for summer's end: there was no better life than reading in repose while in plain sight of flowers and leaves in their full. The cottonwoods were already dropping leaves, he noticed, yellow with blackened edges and cracker crisp. His mother had claimed so that morning, but he'd smilingly chided her about imagining things in her old age. As she read it—and she gave him no hints about her gypsy peering into the future: finger to the wind, canine nose detecting otherwise unnoticed elements of the air, telltale bumps on a cob of corn, who could say?—the dry and hot summer portended a wet winter, though not a cold one. Nothing out of the ordinary, give or take an inch of rain, in short.

Even with its droves of chattering shepherded students, the day had run smoothly. Now, though, he was happy to be bound homeward and on a deserted street. He felt taxed and needful of solitude. Winston could not recall ever speaking for so long and to so many. Confronting the boisterous and chaotic vitality of those teens, he'd been reassured about his turtle's choice of a career. The library was a comfortable shell into which he could retract—that was no shameful fact he kept hidden in an unvisited recess in his mind. It was pragmatic, the most practical of solutions. You don't become a jet pilot if you're afraid of heights, after all.

Years ago, he'd decided that his being librarian would work better for all concerned. It had been a sound judgment. He believed he was helpful and capable when he talked with a single student and assisted him in finding his way through the aisles. An entire class was a different species altogether. Winston had seen so. Disciplining was necessary and he'd developed no taste for it. And all those young people listening to him, regarding him and reacting to his words, demeanor, or dress. Motivated by birds and bees, and whispering comments when he wrote words on the chalkboard. Mrs. Dewwlapp was a running joke, and he could only speculate about what object of scorn or mirth they'd be sure to create from him. He bristled at the picture.

Winston recalled jokes he'd made about a Mrs. Peters when he was in high school, and knew that sort of wordplay was not usually meant to be spiteful. Innocuous or not, it was something he would take care to avoid.

Teaching was a calling, he admitted, but one that beckoned him infrequently. Several days over the year, he sat at the front of the class and administered a quiz or supervised readings when a teacher caught the flu or broke a bone. That suited him fine. It would be an onerous career otherwise. On some days—he'd thought it over a few times—he imagined he would not want to be watched like some actor on a stage, subject to audience whim and its applause, silence—or else figuratively pelted by fruit. And on other days, Winston was certain he would not want to encourage—or even hear, truth be told—half-baked, partially baked, or plainly indigestible ideas about the Cradle of Civilization, *King Lear*, or the Trojan War. He'd concluded that the best teachers pulsated with implacable maternal instinct or else were naturally charismatic; mother-love did not course through his veins—that much was self-evident—and while he was personable enough he possessed none of Svengali's enormous sway. He wanted neither followers nor adversaries.

And he'd come to understand that there was disappointment to take into account as well. Teachers did chortle now and again at the crazy gaffes a student might make. Yet often enough Winston listened as their conversations changed form, growing into resigned-sounding laments about degenerating student quality—each new generation, so went the refrain, offering surer evidence of man's fall from grace. The Nuclear Age of Robotics was upon us, Cameron McKay the science teacher had moaned only last spring while flipping through *Popular Mechanics* at the staff room lunch table, but it'll never amount to much with these feeble-minded car-crazy hooligans at the helm. "It'll turn to rust," he'd said with a doomsday prophet's conviction. He'd snuffed his cigarette with a drawn-out finality, revealing a theatrical streak Winston had never before witnessed.

Nurturing young minds (Mrs. Pierce's phrase) or drilling them (Mrs. Mittchel's disposition): neither held much of an appeal. Books were simple, Winston could say after handling thousands of them, and getting students to find the ones they needed was rewarding without becoming too much of a draw on his personal reserve. Unlike Delilah Pierce, he had only so much to give. It was improbable that he would have ever become one of Father Pourguet's underlings a century ago, spreading the word to the pagan and uncivilized. It was his belief that a man either wants to learn or he does not: no amount of cajoling or force-feeding is going to make him arrive at a place he has no desire to reach.

Winston turned onto his street and stood in front of his house. He'd apparently rushed; even with the cooling weather, he could sense that a fine sheet of moisture had begun to spread on his forehead. As he patted his face with a handkerchief, he looked up. The worn-at-the-edges house he and Alberta mirthfully called Wilson Manor never failed to raise his spirit. Alberta's front yard handiwork of profusely overgrown flowers—hollyhocks, calendulas, zinnias: end of season, a riot of colour and impending rot—greeted him, but caused none of the chagrin his orderly neighbours hinted at with their kindly offers of clippers, mowers, and fertilizers.

He could not count how often he'd been told that the pickets were crying out for a fresh coat of paint. As though the neighbourhood could hear the plaintive wails each and every day. The weathered wood is a nice match for the flowers, sang his mother whenever she encountered one of these help-happy men. Winston had wondered about his mother's actual motivation on occasion, not sure if she'd turned the Manor into a *ramshackle pile*—the insulting term originating across the street—or simply to goad those upright neighbours and their wheedling wives. Alberta admired what she called independent thinkers; when she was in a mood, she grew garrulous faced with their lemming timorousness. "Thou shall paint all pickets white. I must have missed that commandment," she'd huff.

He walked to the side gate. His mother would be with her vegetables.

"Hello, Mother. Is everything as it should be?" Winston said as he trod across the grass toward her.

Alberta was digging around in her dwindling plot of onions. She gave him a little wave and stabbed her pitchfork into the loosened soil. Walking toward him, she held three runt bulbs that swung by their green shoots like tiny pygmy heads. She said, "I think it's time for tea. What do you say?"

She handed the onions to Winston.

"That would be delightful."

Alberta removed her gardening gloves and turned toward the shed. She disappeared for a moment, leaving behind her hat and dirty gloves as she closed the door. With a halting gait she moved across the grass and corralled strands of kinky grey hair that leapt out from her head. She held out her hand and Winston returned the onions.

"Well, another day, another dollar," he said as they started toward the house. Grendel burst from nowhere and raced to the kitchen door.

"Cynical and weary already, my dear? The year's just begun. Surely you've saved a soul already? Helped one of the Wachowski boys find his way to the principal's office?"

It was their habit to mull over the events of Winston's day soon after he arrived home; though she rarely visited him at the high school, Alberta easily recalled the names and personalities her son mentioned. She enjoyed keeping up to date with their stories—some having lunar predictability while others unraveled crazily, like a yarn ball under a cat's fickle guidance.

In the kitchen he told her about the mobile clusters of juveniles and mentioned the boy with the smart aleck question. As she filled the kettle, Winston excused himself. He wanted to see if there was mail—Alberta hadn't mentioned any, so he understood that checking would probably be in vain—and to change out of his stifling work clothes.

Approaching the kitchen from the hallway, Winston saw Alberta stooped near the radio: news at the top of the hour. She lowered the volume when he came near. The newsman's emphatic pronouncements subsided into a murmur. The radio was good company, she said on occasion, as if answering her son's unspoken question about its constant presence. Winston knew she could talk circles around him when it came to current affairs and begrudgingly sought her opinion at election times. He also piggybacked on her handy overviews for use at the library—fairly or not, students approached him as an all-purpose walking-and-talking encyclopedia, equally knowledgeable about Michael Faraday's contributions to science, the territory and foes of the Mesopotamians, and the exact differences between St. Laurent's Liberal and Diefenbaker's Progressive Conservative policies on taxation.

When asked about the latter, he was little more than a parrot for Alberta's point of view. He could never get himself worked up about such matters, particularly since the ancient civilizations—rising and falling between the Tigris and Euphrates; perched for a span of centuries on the Aegean; spreading out like fever across the Mediterranean—held his attention with such a grip. If it turned out that Alberta made an error of fact, then he would blithely repeat it; so far as he was aware, no such lapse had yet transpired: students were not likely to prove him wrong. "Mind like a steel trap," she claimed.

Alberta prepared their tea as Winston drew his chair away from the table. Once he was seated she spoke. "It seems to me," she said, "that young people always dream that any grass must be greener than the dry patch they're stuck on. You know: some great excitement must surely lay in a far away place." She dabbed her forehead with a tea towel: the kitchen always felt a few degrees warmer than the rest of the house.

She lifted the lid and peered into the teapot. After pouring two cups, she carried one to her son. He nodded his appreciation.

Leaning near the sink, she continued with her thought: "Yes, when I was a girl—I was one once, you know—I caught a fancy and sighed for months about leaving for Paris to become a milliner. It was London and dressmaking a few months after that. The ideas didn't seem so far-fetched. Mind you, at the time I hadn't travelled more than ten miles from home. Imagine that!"

He inhaled the smoky steam of his mother's afternoon Lapsang Souchong. She felt that a savory taste was suitable before supper, to whet the appetite. Winston had been taking this blend with her for years, but felt no real love for it; it made him think of burning cedar and smoked salmon. He would have happily exchanged it for another pot of Earl Grey, which he sipped over breakfast on weekends. Alberta held to her rule that it was too sweet for the late afternoon.

"And then you grew up and settled down?"

"I suppose so. The line of least resistance, and so forth. Something like that: the world lets you know that one choice will be more vexing than another." Alberta was roving the kitchen, her cup and saucer in hand.

"That's a nice way of saying it, Mother." Winston raised

his cup to salute her placid coinage. He felt parched; even with the hint of breeze passing through the screen door the kitchen air was hot as soup.

"I seem to recall a period when digging up mummified royalty in the Egyptian sand was how you imagined your future." Hazel eyes squinted as she smiled.

"Yes, that is true, I was smitten alright. Mind you, that had all ended before I was twelve." He could not remember what new aspiration had replaced his dream of archaeology.

"This boy's disdain, though," he said, taking a moment to dunk some shortbread into the tea. "We all might imagine adventure-filled lives, but what was remarkable was that he seemed so contemptuous of home—as though the Bend is little more than a prison to him. I know I didn't feel that and it doesn't sound like you did either."

"You're right, I wasn't running away from home. More like I was drawn to some magical place where I imagined hat makers lived." She topped up her teacup. "But I have no trouble empathizing with the boy, though. You can't call it the land of opportunity here, now can you? Especially if you want to try something out of the ordinary." She walked to the table and grabbed a cookie. "Just think if I had chosen to be a hat maker…. I'm already dangerously close to being the town's eccentric old bat and I never give anyone cause to look twice."

She deposited her tea—half a cookie stowed on the saucer—on the table and picked up the newspaper, reading aloud in her mock newscaster's voice, guttural and low:

"'A local crone, long rumored to be a witch, was burned at the stake by angry berry farmers yesterday evening. They claimed that for reasons unknown she had placed a hex on their crops.' I can see the headline already."

"Oh, Mother." His mother, the comedienne. They remained silent for a moment; ornery crows on the clotheslines broke into squawking conversation.

She picked up her saucer again. "I'm thinking of ham with navy beans and fried potatoes for supper ... though with this heat, potato salad and a few slices of cold ham might be just the thing," she announced, her speculation of a minute before having abruptly reached its conclusion. She'd already moved to the pantry and begun to shuffle through her clutter of jars and bottles. Grendel wound himself between her calves.

Winston told her that he could eat her ham and beans every day of the week. While she prepared it, he'd have time to digest a chapter or two of *Claudius the God*. He refilled his cup, stirred in a half spoonful of sugar, and headed toward the living room.

"Good morning, Mother." Winston walked into the kitchen where Alberta was already at her customary place—back to the counter and arms crossed—at the sink, listening intently to the radio. Sliding his chair away from the table, Winston watched Grendel dart across the floor, dedicated as always to rubbing his shedding coal-black flank against an accommodating set of legs. Her silence encouraged a question: "Not quite awake, Mother?"

"He's to be hanged next week, it's terrible," she said in reply. The newsman spoke of lawyers and a last minute commuting of the sentence before moving on to another news item. Alberta had been following the case intently and felt incensed about the invoking of capital punishment. Mulling it over, Winston held to ambivalence, believing that while the biblical sanctioning of a just, life-for-a-life vengeance seemed draconian, it was also suitable in a case like murder. Particularly, he'd decided, when a man's life was terminated as a result of some asinine emotion like jealousy.

Love gone bad: he'd read that old story hundreds of times and still could not grasp the sudden transformation of rose-scented letters and muttered sweet nothings into a frenzied knife slash across the throat. He didn't flatter himself to think that he was saintly or even deficient in malice and spleen. Murder, though? And not only the sheer brutality; there was the complete thoughtlessness, not a second spent over the numberless repercussions that would ripple like water after a stone's drop. One's life would be permanently off-kilter, another's completely extinguished, and still others turned upside down. Wielding the guillotine or noose or poison pill, though—that was another matter. He couldn't say that he'd hold that much personal conviction. But surely all men should pay for their crimes in full.

Winston had been surprised by his mother's pronounced opposition. It wasn't her habit to become outraged about a complete stranger in a distant city. She'd even spoken out in public, writing letters to the city's paper and the district's politicians. Reading the contents to him—she had hinted that he might spruce up her sentences—Alberta's voice climbed high and became tremulous but fervent in its call for civility. Elegant strings of rhetoric portrayed humanity as evolved and gradually becoming enlightened and the punishment that had been set for Leo Mantha as an unbecoming throwback, a shameful outburst of caveman barbarism and archaic morality. He'd supplied her with *atavistic* and been touched by her generous words. His opinion had not been changed, though. Alberta's picture of violent punishment as an unwelcome vestige of mankind's primitive face was, he felt, evidence of little other than wishful thinking, impractical sentimental hopefulness. He suspected that even one of the tenth graders who pestered him with questions at the library could refute this notion of modern man's supposed civility without too much effort: he'd need only to drag out a few *Life* magazine photographs of Hiroshima, Dresden, and Auschwitz—snapped well under two decades ago—to prove his point.

Winston had no further comments to make about the case and knew the discussion would lead—as it always had—to their long-running debate about mankind's true self. The subject was one about which they stood at sixes and sevens. Like a Cameron McKay who did not fume and rage with disappointment, Alberta believed in progress and gradual improvement thanks to evolutionary leaps: sharper, faster, and increasingly capable as the centuries sped into the future. Winston had aligned himself with a classical conceit. Years ago, he'd read Alexander Pope's couplet about mankind being born on an isthmus between two places—the feral and the angelic—and still felt it was apt. The two qualities were intertwined, fatally entranced by one another like Narcissus and his reflection. It would never change; it was none other than the nature of human nature. No millennia of civilization and supposed evolving were going to alter that fact. How many centuries had passed between Cain's wild murderous outburst and Mr. Mantha's jealous rage, after all? What had changed? Little except for the means of punishment. He'd read, too, about the Id and had no doubt that its throne was an enormous one in the court of man's faculties.

Seated snug against the table, Winston watched his

mother at the stove. Reflected by the prone teaspoon, she was less an elderly woman preparing breakfast than a miniature apparition—the ghost of a moth—fluttering in a fog of silvery light. Rhubarb was stewing; the bubbles released a lemony acrid scent into the warm kitchen air. His tongue gushed juices in response. Passed through the window's variegated vine, the sunlight arrived in lulling tropic hues. Winston thought of poetry. It was a peerless April—irrepressibly sprouting and green, not cruel. He looked down to his foot to check: it was still swollen.

Alberta apparently did not have the heart for a philosophical tussle this morning, and had moved on to her apothecary role. Winston watched as she crumbled sage leaves between thumb and forefinger. With a dramatic flourish—silver bracelets dancing—she released the debris over a bowl, then followed with thick mustard and a pinch each of cayenne and the dried raspberry leaves usually reserved for one of her stomach tonic brews. She lifted the bowl close to her face after swirling the ingredients together.

"That smells about right. This'll fix you up good." Winston heard laughter in her voice; her earlier potions had not worked wonders.

"More voodoo, Mother? Some magic recipe you picked up from your riverbank Indian chums?" Duck egg whites and oolichan oil had been the foundation of her treatment last week. Winston reached down to pat Grendel's flank.

"I'll never tell. What good is a sphinx if she doesn't have mystery?"

Alberta was long used to her child's questions; she'd

smiled at those moments of exasperated disbelief for years. He'd told her often enough that she ought to be consistent, and she'd replied as often that consistency was a sign of a mediocre mind. *Anybody* could be consistent. Mules and ants were consistent.

She placed her remedy on the counter. "Slather some of that on and keep it there for the day. You can tell everyone in the staff room that your dear old mother prepared something delightful and French for dinner and that what they're now enviously smelling are the leftovers."

Heading toward the kitchen's back door, her slow arthritic shuffle was pronounced. Winston told her he expected to be home from work at the usual time. "I'm going to tour the grounds," she muttered. She lifted her grey cardigan from the hook on the door and wrapped it around her shoulders. "That should come off the burner in five minutes," she said at the doorway. Outside, a pheasant's strangled song reported her arrival.

Winston's pale foot was swollen like the white belly of some drowned fish. He'd noticed the ballooned shape while stretched out in the bathtub during the Christmas holidays. Whenever he sank a finger into the soft flesh—the urge to do so was irresistible—he could recall no accident to account for it. He'd let a few weeks pass before showing the appendage to Alberta. Like Winston she'd watched incredulously as her finger pressed slowly into its pillow surface. "It's like clay," she'd exclaimed. They had agreed it must be gout—all those butter-filled breads and sweets!—and decided that a cure would require a restriction of all rich foods. The holiday gorging of dainties must have been the provocation.

And yet even after he'd followed the boiled beef and plain vegetable diet there'd been no change, though both of them had dropped a few pounds. Alberta reported that on the bright side she had noticed a new spring in her step. The foot remained resolute, inflating no further and still not diminishing by an iota. The swelling gave him no pain or discomfort. Still, Winston couldn't help but notice the pinch when he laced his shoe.

Alberta had wondered aloud if the problem might not be *psycho-somatic*, a word Winston imagined she'd picked up in some ladies' magazine. A few years ago, he'd given her a subscription for *Chatelaine* as a birthday present, and she read it—always taking time to mock a sampling of its ludicrous articles—from cover to cover the day it arrived in the mailbox. She'd also explained to him that this word means a physical problem originating with a mental problem, like shell-shock, but hadn't gone so far as to name anything specific. To his sarcastic retort, "Where's the shell-shock in my life, Mother?" she'd raised her eyebrows and said, "You're right, it's as calm as a lake." Later, she returned to the likelihood of gout and began to concoct new herbal remedies that could cure it.

During quiet moments at his library, Winston had speculated with a smirk about the other root—laughably literary—of his ailment. He'd decided that the old Greek story had no relation to him, living thousands of years after the fact and in a wholly different world. That he was living with his mother and that his father was missing was sheer co-incidence. There was no untoward affection here in River Bend City, and, certainly, no lost eye, no oracle, no murder. Even tragedy was a rarity. A drunken murder outside of a beer parlour five years ago was as sensational as it ever got. Not even a perverted crime of passion, like the one that had Alberta so worked up. Small potatoes only. Pathetic failings and petty scrambling for money or territory, those were the headline crimes in the Bend. Nothing tragic or epic. Ordinary, not remotely majestic.

Relaxing in the humid kitchen air, Winston turned his attention to his vexing foot. He held steadfast to his belief that nothing psychological was involved and that there was something else he could do. Poised between his mother's well-intended tonics and poultices and Doc Carter's promissory but inconclusive prescription of *time will tell*, he decided that a trip to a specialist in the city would be the rational man's wisest choice.

A foot doctor's the thing, he thought. He'll discover what's wrong. He'd stop by Doc Carter's and ask for a recommendation.

Winston slid the stewing rhubarb off its element and returned to his chair. He withdrew the problem appendage from a faded brown plaid slipper. The soft skin reminded him of putty. With the same gesture he'd been repeating for months he made an impression of his thumb and then watched it disappear. Without the insulating slipper the linoleum floor was cold, and he walked gingerly to his mother's remedy. He sank a fingertip into the yellow fluid and drew it to his nostrils. Cayenne pepper snuck out from within the mustard's overpowering vinegary miasma. He reached tentatively with the tip of his tongue. It tasted sharp but not unpleasant, as though Alberta had created it to be served with ham and bread at lunch.

Fingers curved into a scoop, he collected some, then crouched and daubed it along the top of his foot just as his mother had instructed. The skin did not absorb the thin ointment, which looked like spilled sauce. With a frown, he scraped off the excess and wiped his hands on a dishcloth. Winston remembered that the egg white remedy had needed to cover the skin overnight. Alberta had told him it might take a while to soak in. He doubted this latest batch of folk medicine would have any more power than the last, but hopped to his bedroom to retrieve a worn pair of socks. If nothing else, applying the poultice helped him feel he wasn't a weak and passive captive of an invisible hunter. The successes of religions and snake oil salesmen were clear to him. Same principle. Winston knew that credulousness was no fire ablaze in his soul and felt glad that his mother's run of curatives had nearly finished.

"I hear that you were going to the city to have that foot of yours examined by a specialist." Mrs. Pierce was reclined on the staff chesterfield, the saucer holding the morning cup of tea poised on her lap.

"You hear?"

"Well, you know. There are no secrets safe in the staff room of River Bend City Senior Secondary School." Winston returned her sly smile.

"I was wondering if I could impose on you? There's this delightful English candy that I have never been able to find out here. I'm sure Eaton's Department Store stocks it."

"Of course, I'd be happy to."

"Delilah tells me you are going to the city to have that foot of yours examined by a specialist." Miss Mittchel sat across from him as he was removing a sandwich from his lunch bag. He'd used the bag so often the paper was as soft as chamois.

"She did, did she?"

"Well, you know. It's well known that there are no secrets safe in the staff room of River Bend Senior Secondary School. I was wondering if I could impose on you? There's this delightful fabric shop that sells a veritable rainbow of embroidery yarns. They stock a Belgian brand that I have never been able to find out here. Jewel colours, remarkable. It is a few quick steps from Eaton's."

"Of course, I'd be happy to."

Winston felt satisfied to reach the address on the map the porter had drawn for him; he was closer still to winning the bet he'd made with Alberta. It was childish, he admitted, but he was filled with a quiver of pleasure in proving his mother wrong. He'd collect the two-dollar bill from her—the clasp of her purse a vise of prudence—the moment he arrived home. And now he'd found the place on his first try. Her prediction had him losing his way twice during the time that he was away.

Craning his neck upward, he imagined the constant stream of ailments that would lead to the building of an entire skyscraper stacked basement to penthouse with doctors' offices, all reflecting what must amount to scores of specialties. Winston wondered whether all the excesses city living paved the way for—hazards and conveniences alike—opened the door to such medical industriousness. And all that close living: population density had been the reason London, England was so devastated by influenza during the Great War. Naïve people sneezing, spitting, coughing, and spreading germs in their sardine-packed neighbourhoods and to myriad strangers on the streets. Who needed goose-stepping Germans to wreak havoc? Beyond the constant city noise and the vertical clutter of buildings, he caught glimpses of soaring grey seabirds and yet greyer water.

He pulled the door open and walked into the veined black marble foyer. Seeing no attendant, Winston found himself excited to be pressing 7 and **DOOR CLOSE** inside the elevator car. He thought of telling Alberta about it and then chastised himself for playing the country hick. "Cripes, it's only an elevator," he said to no one but himself.

The office receptionist was near Alberta's age, though her years of service had rendered her yielding and grandmotherly. An automatic smile hinted at her beneficence. Her familiarity with the room and her job seemed so established that for a moment Winston was gripped by the certainty that this woman was the doctor's mother. She asked him questions gently and filled out the requisite forms with a confident hand, then showed him to a room and requested that he remove his shoes and stockings after indicating the squat leather stool for patients. Winston crossed his legs, but changed his mind and placed both feet firmly on the cool linoleum floor. Instantly tense in the sterile broom closet of a room, he began to count the mottled tiles.

The doctor arrived holding a black wire-spine notepad in his mouth. He nodded to his water glass to mime that he needed the spare hand to open the door. His hopeful raised brow prompted Winston to think of the beleaguered door-to-door salesmen his mother shooed away only after allowing them in to fully pitch their *truly invaluable, Madame* wares. Regardless of what was being sold, she'd inform him, "We had a visit from the Fuller Brush man today," and regale Winston with her story of the threadbare underdog's earnest attempt to scrape together a living. She'd never purchased so much as a pencil.

At times, Winston thought that Alberta seemed little different than a cat that has caught some hapless mouse; she'd draw out the game for as long as it kept her amused. He reminded himself to bring up her vindictiveness the next time she got on her high horse about civility and man's unqualified march of progress. When in the spirit to banter, Winston wagged his finger and asked her to see the bigger picture: that the man had a family to support, she ought to realize, and mouths to fill. "They knock at my door and invite themselves in, so they have to play by my rules," she would never fail to retort. Her statement was a winning strategy.

The doctor withdrew a pencil from the breast pocket of his smock. "Well, you've come a long way, pilgrim," he said, and then told Winston he would try his best to get to the root of the problem. After quizzing Winston about his "medical history" (he'd embroidered needlessly: "that means the physical problems and operations you've had so far, basically"), the podiatrist squatted in front of his patient. He wrapped two warm hands around the bare foot so that the thumbs lay parallel on the veined surface. Winston looked at the man's thick black hair, so carefully parted. It shone with pomade.

Applying steady pressure to the inflated flesh, the specialist compressed it into normalcy, and then, leaning back a few degrees, created a vantage so they could both watch the glacial elastic return. An albino garden slug, Winston thought. Blue eyes beaming through thick lenses, the doctor joked, "Okay, we know you're not pregnant. Otherwise your ankles would have ballooned."

Standing again, the doctor smirked and gave assurances that Winston did not have gout, and then guffawed—"Priceless! Gawd!"—over Alberta's procession of home cures. He smiled with the doctor even though he found the man's familiar joviality at his mother's expense just a touch presumptuous. When Winston could not remember hurting his foot in any way, the doctor explained that it was possible to break one of the tiny bones there without ever guessing, and that in such a case a plaster cast was needless, a self-indulgent luxury. "Time heals all wounds," he announced vaguely, his voice on the edge of jokiness again, eyebrows half way to Groucho Marx innuendo.

"Besides, you should see some of the things that can really go wrong with feet," he said, suggesting that he felt a patient ought to put his lot into perspective. He made notations in the notebook. Winston watched as he wrote *metaplasia?* and heavily circled the word. He wondered whether this young specialist—he couldn't be much older than thirty—had taken a course in modern bedside manner. The man simply glowed with professional confidence.

Winston agreed to visit again after six weeks if the symptoms persisted. The doctor said, "I'll leave you to your socks," and softly closed the door when he left. As he tightened his shoelaces, Winston felt a twinge of annoyance because he'd taken a day off work and made such a large effort for advice he'd already heard. He had imagined in choosing to become a podiatrist the young man would know each and every condition that could blight his patients—and have its cure at hand. At least Alberta had taken measures to remedy it; a saintly waiting for time's healing properties to take effect seemed so pointless: you either got better as a result of medicine or you were defeated. Winston recalled the packages sitting on the dresser in his hotel room. Returning home with Chinese tea, English candies, and Belgian embroidery thread in hand, he thought, there would be three grateful women who would not consider his day in the city completely wasted.

Back in the foyer, the doctor broke away from his breezy conversation with the receptionist and gave Winston's hand a firm shake. Winston liked his heartiness as much as his grooming—he was combed, pressed, and polished with a truly military precision.

Leaving the gleaming black stone foyer of the medical building, Winston wandered and inspected the contents in shop windows, enjoying the Sunday afternoon leisure surely he alone felt on this bustling Friday. He was astonished at the flow of faces and traffic—steady eyes fixed on responsibilities, every man and woman heading somewhere with what looked like important business in mind, opportunities knocking for everyone to hear. Passing by the Granville Street cinemas festooned with midway bulbs, he decided that Mr. Hitchcock and Elizabeth Taylor—or some TECHNICOLOR TREAT in the distance—would have to wait. The hubbub was wearying. He stepped outside the commotion. Back resting against the white glazed brick theatre, he turned his face southward. The huge vertical signs that jutted out—

CAPITOL

PARADISE

PLAZA

ASTOR

ORPHEUM

VOGUE

—brought to mind the plans he and Alberta had made for visiting Las Vegas or Reno. Winston wanted to see desert cacti in bloom and Alberta said she had a yen for some sin: drinking and gambling and Hollywood crooners. Maybe Dean Martin or that little Negro fellow with the glass eye. Failing them: Liberace.

Unlit now, the signs were potent and talismanic, promises for untold thrills once the sun had set. Even the cackling clown's head that invited patrons into the bowling alley arcade below it offered Winston a moment of temptation. He'd never bowled a game in his life. Those run-down lanes in the Bend were for the lowest common denominator. The cigarette smoke alone, he'd heard, could choke a coal miner.

Winston watched as the street's determined throng— business-suited men, errand-running secretaries, lady shoppers with lists to check off—strode with purpose, appearing to have no time for idleness till their tasks were accomplished. Winston thought of ant farms and cooped chickens. In a sense, only the down-on-his-luck rummy he'd passed a few blocks past could be his boon companion. No one else took a minute to dawdle. Winston felt depleted from standing witness to the noise and the city's antic style of living. A catnap would settle his nerves, he decided: he felt brittle as a wood chip. How many blocks would he have to walk? He surveyed the stretch with dismay. Or else—the sudden notion sparked like inspiration—a cup of tea with marmalade and a baking powder biscuit in some quiet corner. He stopped at the *WHITE LUNCH cafeteria*, an establishment that advertised its hospitality with typical city gaudiness: floating above the entrance was an immense yellow neon cup and saucer from which rose strands of white neon steam that flashed bright and then subsided into long periods of dullness. Who could deny its tout's pitch? "'When in Rome,' I guess," Winston muttered. He walked through the double doors.

The hotel's beer parlour was cavernous, but as familiar as any he'd experienced in the Valley—lustrous panels of wood punctuated with mirrors and low lights, the dull murmur of talk, stains, laughter, tobacco, yeasty swill, clatter. Winston knew that he could become a teetotaler with no effort; drink was a social glue for which he'd found little use. He supposed that working men in their Sunday finest had been streaming into this basement to purchase their amber-coloured ticket to bonhomie and oblivion since the days of gas lighting and horse-drawn wagons. Spent years and replenished barrels: as cyclical and enduring as the seasons.

He stood at the entrance and peered into the murky room. At a nearby table, a broad-shouldered man pointed two fingers at his companion sitting directly opposite. Menace was unmistakable in the gesture. Another typical sight, Winston noted. He walked toward an empty stool at the bar and sat at the polished oak counter. As he waited for a harried bartender's "Yes, sir, what'll it be?" Winston grimaced for a moment with discomfort. Out of habit, he'd run the nail of his index finger along a seam in the wood. This reflex test for cleanliness had dredged up a tarry paste that was in fact nothing except accumulated soil from who could say how long ago. He rubbed his fingernail on the side of the stool's mushroom cap cushion. In the mirror he could see that no terrible row had broken out and that the two pals had resumed their drunk-loud banter. In this murky light, he observed, his silhouette was indistinct, one strand in the vast fabric of the crowd.

Ordering a glass of beer, he wondered what gremlin had whispered in his ear to convince him that a drink in a basement filled with men would be a pleasant way to pass the evening. Alberta told him now and again, "Go out and make yourself some friends, it'll do you a world of good," and whenever he went to one of the Bend's watering holes, he returned home in a sour mood, vowing to never again heed Alberta's sibylline advice. She had no idea. The men's easy talk—of sport, work, weather—eluded him. Nor did its slow-witted nods of agreement and platitudinous conclusions truly interest him. Time and again, he concluded that for him such superficial fraternity could serve no valuable purpose. Watching the bartender speedily towel dry a tray of beer steins, Winston calculated that one glass would not take long to finish.

"Hello, sailor. Are you new to port?" The man on the

neighbouring stool leaned toward Winston like a straw-stuffed scarecrow. He smelled bracing if sweet from aftershave.

"I'm from the Valley." Winston remained wary and impassive, catching the man's muted reflection. He hadn't anticipated conversation.

"Surely you have a name?"

"Wilson."

"Richard Williamson. But if you're so inclined, call me Dickie like everyone else." The man swiveled to shake Winston's hand. He smiled: "That's quite a fetching get-up, Mr. Wilson. Is that what they're wearing out in the Valley these days?"

Winston thought to upbraid the stranger for his cheeky innuendo. Turning to address him, he saw a newborn bird for an instant, a hatchling cheeping with hunger, fear, and panic, its eyes blind though calculating. He studied the translucent expanse of Dickie's forehead and noticed shadowy veins. The man appeared delicate and vulnerable, someone with a skull that could be as easily crushed as an egg. Yet Dickie acted any way but frail. He'd have a peacock strut, Winston was sure of it. The uniform sombre suits of the tavern-goers stood in sharp contrast to Dickie's camel coat and radiant silk tie. The man kept his hair—corn silk pale, fine, and thinning—slick with pomade and combed straight back. His eyebrows had been thinned into graceful arches. The man was strange but harmless. Trying to place him, Winston decided that Dickie was dapper, like a preening and silly though possibly malevolent English aristocrat in a

Waugh novel, a creature with station and refinement, if no money. He'd have quite the collection of stories, Winston guessed, and not one about sports or weather.

The conversation between the two men progressed with a sporadic rhythm. Dickie asked elaborate questions laced in suggestion. Winston offered terse answers, occasionally wondering with mild alarm whether Dickie was some kind of con man who planned to bilk him. He pictured his wallet and smiled at the minute pay-off it would give to any misguided swindler. When silence loomed Dickie grabbed for fresh topics—his favourite cocktail, the criminal past of the burly waiter carrying the beer tray, his fondness for sunny Doris Day. He apologized for being *chatty* and yet made no obvious effort to stop. From time to time Winston thought about saying he was tired and needed to return to his hotel room. The man's determination won him over.

"Are you a friend of the Queen?"

"Am I a monarchist?"

"No, that's not exactly what I mean."

There were moments when Winston was reminded of the podiatrist with the jokes in his voice. The nervous man's puzzling speech ran in different directions, making one declaration while insinuating that there were other matters that *could not be made public*, as though Dickie were an anxious spy or an underworld kingpin in some hard-boiled novel with a lurid cover. Trying not to stare at the man's remarkable features, Winston let his eyes wander the room, booming and festive now with sodden conversations. Snatches of song burst from a distant table. He briefly considered that

Dickie might be soft in the head, an example of that odd breed of men who sit at bus depots and café counters and in barbershops and ramble on about nearly anything to anyone within listening range.

After smoothing down his hair with his palms—a completely unnecessary gesture since not a strand had broken free—Dickie made a sudden announcement: "I've got a sight you *do not* want to miss. C'mon." He raised and lowered his eyebrows in quick succession, jokingly and yet persuasive.

Winston hesitated. He could feel the pull of curiosity as well as the force of routine: there was a novel waiting to be read in his hotel room, but it wasn't going to stand up and walk out the door if he didn't make time for it that very night. Besides, the room held no other promise. He could not recall the last time he'd met a complete stranger. Certainly no one in years—if ever at all—had asked him to take a walk in the middle of the night to an unknown destination. The thought that he might be shanghaied bubbled up and burst. Dickie could not be a criminal; the idea was laughable. Besides, what use would they have for a librarian with soft hands? Winston told himself that briny ocean air would be a bracing tonic, and marveled at his sudden come-what-may attitude. His mother might be right about getting out and making acquaintances. Perhaps the only trouble had been the Bend's pool of farmers and loggers.

They hurried along one busy street and then another, Winston a head taller yet hurrying to keep up with Dickie's determined stride. After the first two turns, Winston snorted, knowing he was lost; he had no idea if they were heading toward the Pacific or the Atlantic. Now the bet tipped in Alberta's favour, Winston thought.

At eight p.m., the Bend would have already turned in for the night. The city's neon whir of nightlife exhilarated Winston, though he noticed that the flow of traffic eased considerably as they walked further from the beer parlour. Their footfalls echoed. Past the squat russet block of the Woodward's department store—from a distance its electric **W** rotated silently in the black sky—the city was older and frugally lit. As Winston grew accustomed to the stillness he began to taste the saltwater air instead of the sooty gasoline fumes that poured from cars.

Here, the compact brick buildings were not proud and had little apparent vitality to attract respectable businesses. Winston imagined their rents would be modest, enticing to shady pawnshops and struggling family enterprises. The silent men they passed looked as though they were moving toward no place in particular. Vagrants. With a spinning hand gesture, Dickie indicated that they should pick up their pace.

Dickie proceeded to talk and talk, now effusive and gesturing crazily about any subject. To Winston, the sheer volume of his revelation was incredible. He'd learned more from this man in five minutes than he'd ever heard from Mr. Reynolds, who'd been the principal of the Bend's high school for over a decade. The outpouring was indiscriminate, promiscuous, manic. Dickie lead Winston through the many facets of working in the men's department at the

Hudson's Bay Company department store. His voice became particularly intense when he talked about those customers who treated shop clerks like servants—*I mean, who do they think they are?*—and those nameless others who freely granted themselves *five finger discounts*. And he gossiped mercilessly about the other men and women employees and even revealed the cloak and dagger troubles *upstairs in Management*.

Closer now to Winston, he confided that certain *pervy* customers would try on suits and then make lewd motions while being measured. In a barrage of squints and raised brows and popped eyes, he said there are ways to determine when a man is not wearing proper undergarments. Dickie was obviously at home in this warehouse of salacious details. Winston decided he would have to be careful about what moments from his life he would share with this odd man.

After the career peccadilloes, Dickie diverted the gush of thoughts homeward.

His pets, twin Pomeranians—"the exact colour of cedar chips," he said, and later, "a hellish hue, I swear to God. Right now they're gnawing on the legs of my chesterfield, *I just know it*"—were his pride and yet the very bane of his existence as well. He called them *his brats* and exclaimed more than once that they *need to be taught a lesson*. Their high-strung temperaments threatened to *drive him to Essondale*—and at this moment he shook imaginary iron bars and crossed his eyes as though he already had intimate knowledge of inmate life in that lunatic asylum. No white froth at the corner of his mouth appeared, but Winston would not have been shocked if Dickie's fervor conjured some.

Caught off-guard by the performance, Winston did not know if laughter would be a response his acquaintance would welcome. Dickie described his collection of *objets*, telling his captive audience that such a collection is possible—providing that one is discerning enough—to gather on a modest salary: "You need to train your uncouth eye, that's all."

After Winston told Dickie, "You ought to write a newspaper column called 'Just Ask Dickie.' You should be making money off your ideas," Dickie looked at him askance and retorted, "Are you making a joke?" His tone was cold, as though he'd been subject to a grave insult. Winston decided that Dickie craved attention, not the conversation of equals. He kept mum.

Dickie was describing his plans for a *grand tour* through Europe when he gestured around himself with a flourish and pronounced words that sounded like *Versailles of the Eastside* to Winston's baffled ears. Winston saw nothing out the ordinary, and conjectured that Dickie might be scared and that his animated chatter was his peculiar variation on whistling in the graveyard; certainly the streets had grown emptier and noticeably unkempt. Dickie pointed to the street's oyster shell fragment litter and said that it had been dropped there by gulls. "They're as smart as dogs, you see," was the vague explanation he gave.

Dickie announced that *at long last* they had reached their destination. The Port-Land was no different from the other past-their-prime storefronts on the quiet street. Unprepossessing, Winston thought to say, now there's the best word. He held his tongue. This man had made a special effort to show him a local sight, after all. And besides, the dull brick face might be just that. A front. Winston looked at its undistinguished proportions and weathered paint and predicted a future of broken windowpanes covered by boards and a perennial **For Sale** sign that proved magnetic to no one. Even the Belle-Vu, easily the rattiest tavern in the Bend, gave the Port-Land's forlorn air no competition. The brackish air was its natural complement.

Dickie had claimed he'd never guess their destination, and now Winston conjured a den of sluggish drug addicts. Ladies of the night seemed unlikely. What else could it be? Despite all the talk, Dickie hadn't given him the least peep of a clue. Was there any other possibility? Burlesque dancers? There had been news stories about police raids of narcotic distributors recently. When Alberta did not supply him with the gritty details, he'd read about them himself. That was as unlikely as being shanghaied. The Port-Land's secret identity was an exciting prospect, immensely more so than the absent elevator operator. Mother would love this story.

His eyes adjusted to a room aglow as if lit with dwarf jack-o'-lanterns. Winston sighed at the familiar bar decor—mirrors, wood, stains, the pungent residue of beer and cigarettes—and felt keen disappointment. There were no hoarse and colourful women and not even a single wayward reeling drunk, only quiet men at tables or at the bar bench. Though he had no clear picture how a *junkie* might act, he detected nothing suspicious. A wall of locomotive engine car pictures framed in heavy carved wood was the single unusual element he could spot.

Dickie led him far from the doors to a murky corner near the back wall.

"*Dickie est arrivé*," an arch voice announced.

"Mr. Wilson, may I introduce you to the gang? Clockwise from here"—he gestured with an open palm—"Ed Barnes, then Johnny Schmidt. Our last member is Pierre, though we call him La Contessa with utter respect."

To Winston's eye, Dickie's *gang* closely resembled a motley crew. If the Port-Land was a front, these men gave no clue to its true purpose, looking neither extraordinary nor mysterious. Ed was a chubby drunk, anyone could see it, no doubt acting the foolish delinquent at parties with lamp shade props and off-colour jokes. He was unshaven and had a drinkhound's bleary focus. Johnny reminded Winston of Dickie, ill at ease and fussy. He wore too many rings and had hair heavily laden with pomade. Oily charm and an easy smile, like Liberace in *Sincerely Yours*. Reminiscent of a Saturday matinee gangster, he was shifty-eyed, as though expecting policemen to burst through the doors with tommy-guns ablaze. Older than the other men and wearing a faded and disheveled suit, Pierre appeared to be dozing. The air about their table was thick with aftershave and cigarette smoke. Winston noticed that the table was strewn with glasses, cigarette packages, matchbooks, and ashtrays.

The waiter must be lazy, Winston thought, deserving fewer tips than he already received.

Johnny stood, leaned awkwardly across the table, and offered his hand to Winston. "Welcome aboard," he said.

The table was silent, expectant. Winston, who felt that he had already been speaking for hours if not days, also understood that he needed to say still more. He looked around the room.

"This place is certainly off the beaten track," he remarked.

"Yeah, well.... We've been loitering in this dump for years. It's not respectable but we like it. It suits our needs," Johnny explained.

Ed stood now and extended his hand. "Pleased to meet you, Mr. Wilson. How come we've never seen you before?"

"Call me Winston, please."

"Someone forget to look in the mirror today, Ed? *Charmant*," Dickie interjected.

"You know me, Dickie." Ed's smile was embarrassed.

Dickie turned to Winston. "Ed's a veritable Cro Magnon, been shaving since he was ten. Has to shave his nose, I swear. Honestly, he gets five o'clock shadow at noon." He made a sweeping gesture. "Almost requires a scythe." Winston had already noticed Ed's low hairline.

Winston could not think of a word to add. To fill the silence he uttered a tentative "Oh." He borrowed one of the wooden chairs from an adjoining table and sat down.

"Mr. Wilson is from the Valley. He's practically a farm

hand." Apparently Dickie tolerated lulls for only so long, Winston concluded. He looked around hoping to catch the waiter's eye.

"I'm a librarian, actually. Other than buying the occasional sack of potatoes at the Wong place, I'm afraid I've never been much of a farmer. My mother and I made a deal: she tends to the carrots and onions while I look after the dahlias. Every year we promise ourselves we'll enter the Fall Fair...." He was satisfied that he'd made such a large contribution to the conversation.

"The very salt of the earth, I tell you. There's even a Ma Joad." Dickie couldn't help himself.

Winston turned to address the silent Pierre.

"Don't worry about *her*," Dickie stage-whispered. "She's just taking a wee nap. In her twilight years and all that. Now, Johnny's another story. He came to our very own Terminal City from Winterpeg"—he turned to his subject for a moment—"after a little stay down south in Hollywood." Winston watched Dickie closely. He was puzzled about the man's regard for his friend with the inexplicable nickname. He found Dickie's teasing words distasteful, an obscure insult to the dozing man. And yet Dickie's fondness for him was plain.

"Is that true?" Winston asked. He'd travelled as far south as Seattle and had never seen a tree east of the Rockies.

"Truly, it's Dickie who ought to have jumped on the first train to Hollywood," Johnny said. He waved his cigarette royally—imitating Dickie's grand gesturing—and brushed aside Dickie's sensationalism. "He'd be a natural coming up with scoops for the *Enquirer*. But, yes, it's true I am from the Peg and did spend a few years toiling with the near greats in Tinseltown."

Dickie leaned close to Winston's ear and wrapped his arm around the back of his chair: "And he used to be someone else—he was Dot West way back when." The Port-Land had not been a wasted effort after all, Winston thought.

Dot West was no stranger to Winston. Housewives between Thunder Bay and Victoria would recognize *The Maven of Malkin's Spices* from ten paces way. She was young and shapely and so well organized. It was said her *Kitchen Magic* hints and ideas had saved many a marriage. Her basic philosophy of *Really Tasty Made Really Easy* kept men coming home and children strong and gave women some time outside the kitchen. Even Alberta had used Dot's recipe for Maui Ginger Ribs. Winston had brought a platter of them ringed in halved pineapple slices to a staff Christmas party, and had been happy to return to his mother with glowing reports. When he'd explained to Mrs. Pierce that the recipe had come from Dot West, she'd nodded, "You can't go wrong with her. You simply cannot. She's such a smart cookie." She'd asked Winston to remember to bring her a copy of the recipe.

"Let me set things straight, alright? The whole truth, so help me God." As he spoke, Johnny leaned in too, playing up the mock conspiracy. "We had the Art Department sketch us a housewife for our Age of Convenience, nobody too chicken feathers countrified and not too hoity-toity either, a housewife with a little extra going on upstairs. You know?"

Johnny tapped his temple. Grabbing his beer, Johnny drank until the glass was drained. He lifted his hand to signal the thick-necked waiter. As the man barrelled toward their table, Winston could see that the true talent of this gruff man would shine whenever a brawl broke out. With a slow circling finger, Johnny ordered another round. The waiter returned promptly with a replenished tray. Coarse but familiar: "Here you go, ladies." Hearing such slang used by the waiter—not a man of many words, clearly—Winston guessed that like many of the ridiculous expressions uttered by pupils over the years, this citified one would be long forgotten in five years' time.

Johnny handed him a stack of coins. "Thank you kindly," Winston said. Holding up his beer, Johnny nodded a toast. His inky eyes were set and intent. Winston couldn't imagine what those intentions might be.

Johnny offered the Camel package to Winston and then lit a cigarette. He spoke again after he exhaled. "So," he said, leaning back on his chair, "I named her Dot because it's simple, clean, and easy to remember. The company's market stretches westward to the Pacific from Winnipeg, so West seemed like a sure bet. That was the concept: a domestic goddess for Western Canada, or some damn thing. Then, at the head office we hired some pretty young wife from Saskatoon to be our Dot in ads and to make public appearances now and again at Malkin's or sometimes at department stores. We had her take trains out for parades in cities; she tossed little spice canisters from atop the Malkin's float. Anyway, she just followed our cues; couldn't boil an egg to save her life. The household magic was lifted from women's mags and fancied up a bit. And every recipe was my own."

Winston imagined that Johnny was used to speaking to roomfuls of executives in order to pitch ideas. His style of speaking was not hypnotic so much as melodic. The rolling cadence drew the listener in naturally.

"She really caught on. We thought that we could really capitalize on that popularity, use her as a house brand"— he stopped to swallow some beer—"you know, Dot West Creamed Corn, Dot West Peas. Her pretty face beaming from every damn place. Then the higher ups at Westfair Foods thought Dot had run her course and cleared out the PR department. Of course, they've kept her going since I left. I gather they're going to phase out that campaign more slowly than they had originally planned. Or maybe they just wanted to trim some fat and get rid of us creative types. Pared us right out of their payroll, that's for sure."

Listening to Johnny, Winston felt once again like a rube. Along with Mrs. Pierce, he had thought of Dot West as a capable woman, remarkable—an actual woman to admire—because she was able to organize herself so well that she could have the extra time—and pluck—to tell a company like Malkin's about her recipes and household ideas, and then sign a contract with them. What a sham. It was like being dazzled by Santa Claus because he could reach all those chimneys during one night. Only children and half-wits can do so for long.

"And you went to Hollywood after that?" Winston asked. Beneath the nervous wariness, Winston was pleased to find Johnny's charm.

"Oh dear, we've heard this soap opera before. Don't get him started. There'll be a river of tears here in no time," Dickie interjected.

Johnny said, "If you visit our fair city again, Mr. Wilson, I'll tell you a story of powerful and glamorous men and women and of gut-wrenching despair." Winston smiled at the radio play melodrama.

"Count me out, fellas," said Dickie, evidently feeling left out of the limelight.

"Richard." Johnny was getting angry.

"Let's change the topic before you two make a scene," Ed said. Husky yet small-featured, he uneasily surveyed the room. Clearly timid, he smiled and said nothing else. He rotated his pinkie ring when he spoke.

"With the exception of the timid tortoise here"— Dickie's glance at Ed was not kind—"we're born tellers of tall tales here, Winston."

Winston could not guess whether Dickie planned to unravel a story. After long seconds of silence, he prompted Dickie. "I see," he said.

"In fact, when he's had a few too many, even Ed here will describe hair-raising scenes from some of our city's finest establishments," Dickie said, looking around and then leaning toward Winston. "He's one of the inspectors for the Liquor Control Board. He makes reports, you see, and jots down what goes on behind closed doors. And it's not only bug infestations and watered-down booze like you'd expect. It's scandalous. Far worse than all that."

Winston had never before dedicated a second of thought

to the secret lives of cocktail lounges and beer parlours. Were they like Dot West, something other than what they appeared? After hearing Dickie's revelations about perversion and managerial backstabbing at the Hudson's Bay, he guessed it was possible; nothing was impervious. Winston felt suddenly eager to hear vignettes of cocktail lounge confidential.

But the silence hinted that now was not the time for Ed's revelations. Winston turned to the silent Contessa. He lurched slightly, eyes still closed.

Winston was unable to keep pace with the thoroughbred conversationalists who surrounded him. He felt tongue-tied. As always that trait worried him; but he soon discovered that while he was frequently the object of attention— "Hush now, we'll give the farmer a bad impression," "Listen up, Hayseed"—he needed only appear alert and engaged. It was enjoyable listening to the racy talk that cemented their strange fraternity. The experience was reminiscent of sitting in a movie theatre and watching outlandishly bad characters interact with supremely heroic ones. Part of the pleasure came from knowing that their moral extremes bore little relation to the daily life of ordinary men.

Besides, Winston could feel that his throat was scratchy from all the cigarette smoke; speaking at their rate would render him hoarse in short order. He envisioned them transplanted to the staff room and smiled at the quiet outraged responses they'd inspire. Mrs. Pierce would be beside herself, huffing and completely outgunned.

"Well, we'd better get you back to your hotel before they lock up this town and throw away the key." Dickie was already sliding back his chair so that he could stand. "Okay, boys, it was *enchantant* as ever. I'll be seeing you."

Winston followed. "It was a pleasure to meet you all. Depending on my foot, it may be that we'll meet again soon."

"The pleasure was ours," Johnny said intently, then smiled. "See you, Hayseed."

"*Au revoir.*" Pierre's eyes remained closed as he mumbled the words, "To be divine is your task and mine."

Ed stood and shook Winston's hand energetically.

The air outside was brisk and sharp with seashore decay. The breeze had picked up. Dickie told Winston that they would never find a taxicab; had they chosen to, they could have walked along the middle of the street without a single car passing them by. After he assured his guest that the fifteen-minute walk would be over in no time, Dickie offered up no additional words.

"Ed's a bit of a lush, hey?" Winston said, trying on Dickie's cattiness for size.

"He's a close friend," Dickie said. "I prefer not to speak of him in that way. He can't help himself; he's had a tough time of it."

Winston waited, thinking that Dickie was soon to launch into a fresh salvo of gossip. A dead or delinquent child maybe, lost jobs, or a wife who'd cruelly abandoned him. Dickie chose to elaborate no further.

"I'm sorry, I didn't know." That was all Winston could think to say.

"It's nothing. We go a long way back, that's all."

Winston felt confused like a bounding breed of dog with a master who let him roam free and then abruptly kept him tightly leashed. He was itching for Dickie to entice him with another story of epic misdeeds, but could never guess when one might surface.

"It's their benediction, in case you're wondering."

"Pardon me?" Winston was relieved, glad to offer encouragement.

"The Contessa belongs to the Queen For A Day Club, and corresponds with other winners in the States. When they have their luncheons they chant, 'To be divine is your task and mine' before they eat."

"But how can he be ... a Queen?" Winston imagined he was getting entangled in Dickie's double entendres.

"Well, that's a funny story, actually. He had a neighbour, some frumpy tragedy named Mrs. Claribel Spivak—that was her name, honest to God—who won a few years ago, before when it was on the radio only. It was the usual miserable story: flat broke, brats and bills and a loser of a husband who drank away their money and got rough when things didn't go his way. Maybe she had goiter and gallstones too, I can't remember. Anyway."

Dickie was enjoying drawing out the details, Winston could see. He had grown animated once again as he recalled the dregs of this woman's marriage, creating cartoon pantomimes of the feckless husband guzzling from a bottle and children bawling in feverish rages. They walked in halting steps along Hastings Street, Dickie stopping now and again to look in windows of ladies wear shops and jewellery stores or else pausing to emphasize an element of the La Contessa biography.

"The applause-o-meter was loudest after she trotted out her disasters, and so Mrs. Spivak got the grand prize. Must have been a slow week, I suppose. A few weeks later some ancient American relic who was a Queen in 1948 or something wrote to her and said she was eligible to join their special Club. Mrs. Spivak didn't read so well and brought the letter to the Contessa. He explained it to her and offered to write back and see what benefits Spivak might get from belonging." Dickie slowed his pace and looked directly at Winston. "But then—and here's the kicker—Mr.-Spivak-the-boozer sold her things and abandoned his Queen of Misery. She couldn't even make the rent and did a midnight move herself, kids in tow. The Contessa wrote back anyway and decided to play at being Mrs. Claribel Spivak for a while, sort of a member by proxy. He was even the Club's Treasurer for a year. He sent a photograph of his mother to them after they asked for a memento for their scrapbook. Now, I think that when she's had a few too many, the Contessa's living through a little Club luncheon in her mind."

"That's incredible. You gentlemen have *lived* so much more than I." Winston felt as though he should say so, but he wasn't entirely convinced.

As Winston reached familiar sights at Granville Street,

he felt himself being comforted by the sight of traffic, lights, and occasional after-hours revelers. The scarlet scallop promoting **SHELL** oil was radiant, a beacon that served no purpose other than announcing its being at the very centre of things. The clock faces below, glowing hotly, warned latecomers in four directions. Winston was tired out. He realized that at his advanced age his taste for adventure had diminished. Not that he'd been much of a rebel when he was young. Still, an evening spent in the company of those eccentric men would become valuable, a curio for Alberta and something he could recall fondly whenever he chose. It was like nothing he had ever done before.

"Here you are, Mr. Wilson." Dickie's upturned palms meant "*Voilà.*"

Winston slowly surveyed his hotel, ground floor to roofline. "Well. That was quite an experience, Dickie. I can honestly say I have never occupied an evening quite this way."

"I aim to please, you know." Dickie had to speak more loudly than usual because he'd stepped back from the hotel's main doors. "I have the feeling we'll be seeing you soon. Ta-ta." Dickie turned away without the flourish Winston had come to expect. Winston watched until he disappeared around a corner, and then walked inside the brightly lit lobby. With a start, Dickie's exclamation *I've got a sight you do not want to miss*, came to mind. The Port-Land could not have been the promised sight, Winston imagined. Perhaps Dickie was waylaid by that impromptu visit with his friends and they'd never arrived at the actual destination. It didn't matter, Winston thought. The evening had been an adventure all the same.

They strode down the empty halls, a gaggle of professional talkers now keen to begin one of their last get-togethers before the summer vacation. Close to Winston, Delilah thanked him once again for being so obliging with her special requests. She spoke quietly: "I don't mean to impose, and yet that is what I seem to be doing whenever I walk through your door."

Only after gathering in the staff room did the assembled teachers realize their cramped sanctuary—chock-a-block with two chesterfields of advanced years and an assortment of mismatched chairs, tables, ashtrays, and cups for tea and coffee—would not serve them well. Cameron McKay suggested his classroom with its broad plain of black-topped work stations cluttered with sinks and Bunsen burners. "Plenty of surface area, it'll do the trick," he said, already standing up to leave.

They strode down the empty halls, a gaggle of professional talkers now keen to begin one of their last get-togethers before the summer vacation. Close to Winston, Delilah thanked him once again for being so obliging with her special requests. She spoke quietly: "I don't mean to impose, and yet that is what I seem to be doing whenever I walk through your door."

The Curriculum Committee had been asked to produce a list of recommended books for the new Family Life Education unit that would start up in September. Delilah had explained that the committee needed to act with haste since it had left this matter until so late in the year. She reminded him that he did not have to help them to make a decision, but his expertise with the materials and overview of their merit would be thoroughly welcome.

Winston could hear McKay's one-way conversation with dimple-cheeked Mrs. Pratt, the chubby Guidance Counselor whose flat expression and perennial drab woollens belied her happy-go-lucky disposition. Winston turned to see Mr. Westburn talking to his wife Mary and Miss Mittchel. It was plain that the Vice-Principal was telling them a joke; the man lived for them, or so he liked to say whenever Winston stood within earshot. Like whistling and gum chewing, joking was positioned high on Winston's list of unsavoury characteristics.

Now McKay was grumbling about woeful parents ("They should be required to get a license") and the School Board's passing the buck yet again.

"Who will teach the darned course?," he asked. "You? Miss Mittchel in Biology? Phys Ed? Ought we to bring someone in?" The enthused voice dragged in Winston and Delilah.

"We used to have that dour nurse lady from the Canadian Social Hygiene Council come in. Delilah, you remember Mrs. Pitt, don't you? She was like a Sherman tank or that sour Salvation Army matron who rings her bells in front of Eaton's over the Christmas holidays. She did fine work, I imagine. No nonsense." While talking he had scurried ahead of the group and now walked backwards to address them.

Delilah was agreeable. "I'm sure she did, Cameron. I think the School Board is looking for something more comprehensive and more, well, secular. Perhaps Mrs. Pitt was too admonitory." As though buffeted by a sudden gust, she patted her blonde hairdo.

"And by that you mean?" McKay asked, stock still. He was testy; time and again, he'd explained that two-dollar words made his hackles rise.

"You know precisely what I mean, Cameron. We have been through this before. It's not a Sunday school lesson." Winston recognized her pursed expression: it was all-purpose and he'd seen it manifest when students made atrocious excuses for not handing in homework assignments and in the face of inclement weather. Once, soured milk in the staff room refrigerator had brought it on.

At the door to the Chemistry classroom she stopped and withdrew a sheet of paper from her file folder. She cleared her throat and addressed the impromptu assembly:

"Here are the words we underlined in the report that the School Board sent to us—

<u>moral standards</u>

<u>delinquency</u>

<u>social diseases</u>

<u>prevention</u>

<u>hygiene</u>

<u>family science</u>

<u>citizenship</u>

And let's not forget that there was the request, in italics no less, that *'girls and boys should receive scientific education about the origins of life, their responsibility for life, and social standards.'* It's these ideas we must sift through. Do you recall now, Cameron?"

"No hellfire, in other words," Winston said, directing the conversation back to Mrs. Pitt's shortcomings. He felt thankful that he had steered clear of committee work. Enmity and groups always seemed to walk hand in hand.

Winston was familiar with the Board's goals. Weeks before, Delilah had spoken to him about her ideals for the unit: "the introduction of proper attitudes, high standards of moral conduct, the development of a healthy, sober, and moral attitude toward matters of sex"—she had pronounced the word gingerly—"in general."

They sat around two lab tables near the open windows. The breeze that came in smelled of grass clippings and lilac. Delilah, the chairwoman of the committee, spoke once everyone had settled on his wooden bench seat. "We will strive to make our selection today, but before we begin my special guest Mr. Wilson will give us his summary of the materials already in our library."

She clapped her hands in welcome and then turned to Winston. "As you are aware, Winston, our concern is with obtaining modern books that have no undue salaciousness. We are going to be teaching teenage boys and girls who take anything the wrong way. What do you have for us?"

"Well, the library's locked-up material really doesn't add up to a mountain. It's barely a molehill. A few volumes are relics from the reign of King George V. I can assure you that they're just curiosities."

He held up a tattered brown book and passed it to Delilah. "Still, there is *Healthy Living: Principles of Personal and Community Hygiene.* It dates from nearly four decades ago, but it's interesting and discusses everything except the kitchen sink: from caring for baby to preventing hookworm. And it has useful homework questions at the end of each chapter: 'Why is picking the nose a dangerous as well as an unpleasant habit?,' for instance." Guffaws were followed by colourful anecdotes about poor student hygiene.

"The author is from the Yale School of Medicine. He does go on a bit, though. And it's two volumes as well. That could get expensive. The book could be out of print, even. I rather enjoy this one particular volume because some aspiring Browning has included her verse in big loopy letters—

> *Fall into the river from*
> *off the deck,*
> *Fall down stairs and break*
> *your neck.*
> *Let the glittering stars*
> *fall from above,*
> *But never, never fall*
> *in love.*

"Awfully cynical for one so young, I'd say, but it might be the best sort of principle for students here in the Bend. Caveat emptor."

"*Principles of Personal and Community Hygiene*. Sounds socialistic," McKay offered. No one answered his challenge.

"Let's see, what else is there? *Growing Up Emotionally* and *Facts of Life and Love for Teen-Agers* were written specifically for young people, and feature the kinds of questions a juvenile would supposedly ask. They're pamphlets, really, and a tad basic.

"Some things—I am not at all certain how they found their way into our high-minded library—are too detailed and racy. Published in Germany, *The Key to Love and Sex (in Eight Volumes)*, for instance, has explicit content. It does come in eight volumes, though, some more salacious than others, and they're thin and modestly priced. There's *They Stand Apart*, which is only about perversion from a legalistic perspective." Winston was surprised when a picture of Leo Mantha hanging from the gallows coalesced before his eyes like a dream image. It lasted for the briefest of moments. "For both, I imagine parents would complain about the permissive attitude. In addition, the details might open a can of worms for inquisitive minds." He handed Volume 4, *The Abnormal Aspects of Sex*, to Delilah and Volume 2, *Historical Attitudes Toward Love and Sex*, to the English and Western Civ teacher, Mary Westburn.

"Both *Attaining Manhood: A Doctor Talks To Boys About Sex* and the *Attaining Womanhood* companion volume are matter of fact and informative. There is not too much technical terminology, but it is scientific. There's nothing salacious at all. Nor socialistic." He smiled toward Delilah. "And they are illustrated." He gave both slim grey books to Cameron McKay.

"Finally, there are some movie reels: *Social-Sex Attitudes in Adolescence*, *The Meaning of Adolescence*, and *Physical Aspects of Puberty*. I didn't look at them, but I'd hazard that the last is more perfunctory than the others. Obviously, they should be secondary or supplementary."

"Oh, yes. Mrs. Partridge must have heard about this meeting because she stopped by and gave me a copy of her Home Economics textbook." He held up the last of the books in his stack. "This brand new *Junior Homemaking* is fine, but it is really just a textbook designed to help girls become good housewives—if 'How Pretty Can You Be?' and 'Are You a Household Treasure?' are chapter titles we can judge by. It ought to remain in Home Ec."

He handed that heavy volume to Mrs. Pratt, who flipped through the pages intently. An instant later she snapped her fingers. "Perhaps we could comb through the books and type up our own booklet, one that's suited to our needs here. It would certainly not be costly. And that way there'd be no extraneous material."

"Are you volunteering your time?" At that moment, it was obvious to Winston that Cameron McKay joined committees because he was a bully. His natural prey were sheepish do-gooders like Delilah and Betty Pratt, gentle women, he imagined, who wouldn't put up much of a fight.

"If we worked together, it'd be done in no time," was her spirited reply.

Delilah thanked Winston for his efforts. She spoke to the others and then told him that they had some decisions to make. "Now's when the fun begins, Winston. Naturally, you may stay if you like, but I have the feeling that we will be burning the midnight oil." Her face pinched for an instant as she settled her eyes on Cameron McKay. She'd give Winston the inside story during her recess in the morning, he could guess.

"As much as I'd welcome the chance," he said, sliding from the bench, "I should get home, check in on Mother. I'll get those books back from you tomorrow. There's no rush, though, if you'd like to keep them a while longer. Good luck."

In the first week following his visit, Winston was a dedicated student of the specialist's thumb press technique. Arriving home from school each afternoon, he'd eagerly take off his shoes and socks filled with the hope—ridiculous, and he knew it—that the doctor's hazy prognostication would correspond to some visible change: mind over matter. When that fleshly material proved resistant, he decided that as a diagnosis *Time heals all wounds* was sketchy enough to become the byword for turbaned clairvoyants at midways near and far; they could adopt it as a handy alternative to "A loved one is concerned about you." Really, what was the use of saying it? Death would drain his foot, no doubt. And that was only a matter of *time*. Anything and everything was a matter of time.

After that one obstinate foot failed to obey his will, he began to give the pair of them a nominal inspection in the morning. Practical choice won over speculative hand-wringing: he'd discovered that he could avoid discomfort altogether by wearing his usual black wool sock on the normal foot and a silky one, thin as onion skin, on the other. Weeks later, daffodils and narcissus having bloomed and wilted, the difference between the two remained exactly the same, ropy and skeletal on the left, bloated as a drowned man on the right. The doctor had said in so many words that what he saw was barely worth fretting over, and now Winston resigned himself to that learned opinion. There were many worse problems in the world, he lectured to himself. This one was peanuts. He felt relief when he thought how different it would be if he had woken up with a face that was half inflated. Or suffering from a blinding headache that kept him secluded in a sunless room.

Winston dutifully swabbed on pungent salves until Alberta became resigned as well. She tried out a few new combinations—an odd ingredient like catnip or fish roe swirled in with the standard dollop of mustard—and then snorted at her fruitless determination: "Ha! What's next, prayer? A visit to a faith healer?"

It was a perplexing condition, but her mirthful fancies about it induced a bout of laughter. While rifling through her herb drawer—you really ought to organize this godawful jumble of envelopes, jars, and paper scraps, she repeated the resolution for what might be the hundredth time—on a May morning filled with the threat of a scorching summer, she poked fun at the idea of them making some Old Testament-style pilgrimage to a wind-whipped canvas tent. Her vision relocated them to an endless dry grass field in the Prairies rather than a desert in the Levant, and arriving by bus.

She piled up the details: they'd have to wait in a long

queue and talk to other travel-cramped desperadoes—a tired, lank-haired woman with a heavy-set, simpleton daughter; a recently married couple whose only child had been paralyzed by polio—about their pain and anguish and pretend to have faith in their capricious God, who had first stricken them and then offered up an unlikely map back to health that had led them to a scorched plain in the middle of nowhere. She'd have to hold her tongue, she imagined, yet she'd be granted the rare opportunity to watch her son being forced to pass the time in dreary talk with complete strangers. Chewing the fat. Crops, weather, sickness, and God: Oh, how he'd squirm.

As Alberta widened the vision's scope, its mugging vaudeville callousness faded; she concluded they'd be on the first bus to Reverend Whatshisname if her son became sick and no one could help him. It was a mother's right. Why wouldn't she? Chiding herself for such mawkishness, she thought, I've grown into a weepy old woman. She blanched when she pictured herself as one of those fussy Orange Pekoe-sipping ladies who spend their long days looking with wistful, tear-brimmed eyes at old photographs and whispering of war and fateful, misery-bringing letters from the government. Stuck so deep in the mud of the past, she huffed.

Alberta abandoned her brewing of remedies and talk of shoring up her store of knowledge. There was a time when you stopped darning holes in a sock, after all, and threw it in the bin. And, besides, there was nothing left to use in that musty drawer. No alchemical combination. She held fast to her conviction that a cure was out there, hanging on to that certainty without qualm, and spoke to Winston now and again of holding a pow-wow with the Indians who sold bargain salmon at shadowy cottonwood groves along the river's bank. It was just that there were better ways for her to spend her mornings than fretting about proportions and herbs. With her gardens, for instance.

Besides, it wasn't as though her son's malady was any more serious than the various aches and swellings that afflicted her each and every season. She had long since given up on remedying her patches of scaly skin—even after valiantly trying grandfather Wong's remedy of abstaining from potatoes for two entire months, during winter. ("Too much heat" was his slow-coming explanation.) Now she would do the same with a swollen foot. Oh well, what can a soul do but try? It didn't warrant all her doting—she believed that living through children like some kind of leech was no better than staring mournfully at dusty old photographs. The whole she-bang was in fact easy to forget about: he didn't limp or complain and was not in the habit of parading around barefooted.

"*C'est tout*," she said to Winston one morning when he asked about the contents of her latest concoction. "I'm about to make a batch of cheddar scones, so it's flour in the bowl this time. I thought I'd make your coffee first. That okay?" Winston was surprised that Alberta would admit defeat so soon. He thought to feel slighted—his own mother giving up on him, was nothing sacred?—but reminded himself that he had no real faith in her brand of medicine.

"I wonder when," he muttered. He crossed the room and ran an index finger along the days of the kitchen calendar. Having finished percolating Winston's coffee, Alberta was measuring leaves for her morning pot of tea. Grendel was stretched out at her feet; Alberta had dropped him a few dried catnip leaves, and after a spasm of activity the cat had settled into a euphoric slumber.

Winston spoke to her from across the room. "Mother, this is going to be another permanent feature on me, like weak eyesight or dandruff in winter. It doesn't hurt, it doesn't change, it's simply there. Nevertheless."

"That's what I said when my hair began to thin out. 'It's just there,' or not there in my case, I suppose. Anyway, you'll always notice it," Alberta held up an imaginary hand mirror and squinted. "I'm just a Gorgon without the snakes."

"Oh, Mother."

"You're going to take another trip to the city?"

"I may make a weekend of it. See a show or two. Get you some more of that Lapsang Souchung, even though I can't fathom why you drink the noxious smoky stuff. Say, why don't you come along? *We* can make a weekend of it."

"Now there's an idea, though it's spring and I've made the switch out of Lapsang. Of course." Her tone was snappish, suggesting that Winston was dumb as an auk. "But you're right, we could make a weekend of it. It's been too long since this old girl has done anything except slave at the stove." Winston thought his mother was tart and vinegary this overcast morning.

With lips pursed and arms crossed, he turned to her.

"You poor so and so. Well, I hereby grant you manumission. For one weekend only, mind you. Today's your lucky day." Winston realized that it had been years in fact since he and Alberta had spent a frivolous weekend away from the Bend. They talked of packing their luggage and taking a train or bus somewhere, but the actual trip never seemed to materialize.

Alberta improvised an African genuflection. "O massuh, you da bestest massuh evuh."

Fully grinning, he returned his attention to the calendar. "I'll have to make a long distance call to the hotel and doctor this time. Let's hope there's a space in his appointment book."

She walked to the sink and stared out the window. She exclaimed, "Well, I'm going to have to air out my glad-rags. At the very least. They've been stuffed in a corner of my closet so long they are as wrinkled as all get out—I don't even have to look. Let's hope there's no mould and that the moths haven't had a field day."

"You're turning into quite the city slicker." He looked up to see Delilah at the library's front door.

Delilah's being finished earlier than him was a rarity. She arranged regular meetings with students in order to keep up to date with their progress. It added an extra half-hour to her daily schedule, which Winston usually reminded her of when he was leaving for home. Today, he'd needed to spend some extra time on book orders. The restrictions of the budget had him feeling tetchy.

"I bet you've found some sweetheart," she said with a false smile.

"Yes, you've figured it all out, Miss Marple. Congratulations. You'll be the first to get an invitation. We're thinking of a spring wedding." She'll be a spinster in no time if she doesn't watch herself, he thought after she'd quietly shut the door. Exposure to city life might do her some good.

During April's trip to the city, Winston had scarcely looked up from *Memoirs of Hadrian* over the two hours the train took to reach the spectacular Pacific terminus. He'd known what lay beyond the coach's window; the salmonberry bushes, cow pasture, and muddy river water were as unremarkable as zucchini in August. And he'd encountered gossips like the pair of downtrodden scavengers who'd sat across from him often enough to appreciate the value of a book. It acted as a charm to ward off evil. He'd considered those women in their faded calico, and concluded that the hero of his novel really was a deity. Publius Aelius Hadrianus. Now there was someone with a story worth paying attention to. He'd thought it was sad that dignity and heroism were so easy to locate in literature and yet such a rarity in daily life.

Travelling with Alberta, though, he would not be given a chance to read anything, not even a newspaper. She said as much, the excitement seeping from her voice: "You're not going to read now, I hope?" They sat facing one another. Alberta had placed her bags and gloves on the adjoining seat; Winston's folded coat and hat were covering his. The novel rested on his lap; his index finger was wedged in where he'd left off.

"Since you made us trudge down to the station like hobos, planting myself here and relaxing strikes me as ideal. Sheesh, how many miles was that?" Winston fixed his attention on the book's cover.

"But there's so much to look at."

"What do you mean? There's nothing whatsoever out of the ordinary." He swept through the scene outside with a quick dismissive glance.

"Look at the trees. They're luminous, as green as they get. And the river is more swollen than your foot can ever be." Alberta was speaking from memory apparently, because she was bent over removing her shoes.

"Yes, O Empress of the Wild. Maybe Princess Stop and Smell the Roses should spend less time with her Indian friends. Besides, there was plenty of nature in ancient Greece. Olive trees, grape arbours, and hemlock galore." He waved the book at her. Winston could think of nothing he'd prefer at this instance. He'd moved on to *The King Must Die*, but was still finding Theseus a bit stagy. All those pages of Attic speechifying, it was hammy. The novel was bound to improve.

"To raise such a cynic of a child. What ever did I do wrong?" Having finished unfastening her shoes, Alberta's face remained fixed on the outdoor scene.

"You didn't keep me in your papoose long enough, I suppose, Mother Nature. We're going to be incinerated by the sunshine in about five minutes, so maybe we should just pull down the blind." He stood and began to reach for the dangling cord.

"Don't you dare! So cheeky!" They were both smiling. The bantering was their comic routine—as old as any of their shared memories. They both relished it and exaggerated their differences for the sport.

"You know, whenever I'm on the train and it's level with the water and the water is leading toward the sea, I always imagine this place before we were here." Having lost the contest of wills, Winston had already placed the book on his coat.

"The Wilson dynasty? Or are you referring to the time before Cook and Vancouver and grubby gold rush miners?"

"I mean when animals ruled the world. Nobody else. Well before the age of cities. It's something of a mix-up because a few mammoths are roaming as well as some dinosaurs—I have a peculiar fondness for the brontosaurus, so always throw in a few. No people, though, not a soul. It all seems majestic..." She stood up to get a better view of the scene outside the window. "...and awesome."

"So much poetry and so early in the day, Mother." He understood Alberta's point but did not feel it. "I'd rather see a painting of it, something by Emily Carr maybe. In an art museum. Anyway, Oscar Wilde said that art is an improvement on nature. If I were stranded beside you in your prehistoric wonderland, I'd be looking for the nearest exit out. There's something about wide-open spaces swarming with reptiles that has me craving art and craft—central heating, a cozy armchair, and a good novel."

"Oh, you. Small wonder we never go camping. Biscuit?" She reached into her embroidery bag and began to unfold a waxed paper parcel. Their car rolled by vibrant stands of salmonberry and cottonwood.

Winston decided that it was Alberta's enthusiasm at leaving the Bend that had been the catalyst for her impromptu lecture about life before apes and civilization. It was a romantic, noble-savage diorama she drew for him, but minus even the savage. Truly, she had painted a big primitive pastureland, one with far more grazers than predators. Edenic—for a cud-chewer.

"And how do you imagine surviving in this place, Mother?" He tried out her idea; removing the links of log booms from the river, he imagined something like an Ogopogo heaving its sleek eel's head out of the muddy current.

"That's not the point. It's a bit like visiting a ranch. Only I am invisible—or at least nothing spots me—and just watch them peacefully go about their business. Lovely."

"Lonely, I'd say. And anyway there's no intelligence there, Mother. Animal instinct only! And that means there is no culture. It's all packs, flocks or prides, and being led around by some elemental pulsations: go forth and multiply. Eating, sleeping, mating until they're feeble and then melt back into the earth." Winston was intrigued by her creation.

His need to respond was habit rather than dismay.

"Porter." Alberta spoke out over her son's head and raised her hand to wave. Winston watched her silver bangles slide up her forearm. An elderly man, stooped and turtle-paced, made his way toward her. "How long will it be before we arrive?" He checked his pocket watch, and was sure to explain that his answer was "an approximation." Winston pictured a troupe of porters in a train station office being given a pep talk by their higher ups, explaining how they must use that phrase so that nobody could complain if the train was running late.

He returned to his station at the end of the car after asking, "Is that everything, Madame?" Alberta was trium-phant: "You see! He answered me because he sensed that I am higher than he is in the pack and should be obeyed. There was no intelligence there, just instinct. Ha. That's your civilization. It's nothing except that, but it dresses itself up, puts on airs. La-dee-da." She made the hand gestures of a fine lady lifting her skirts to take a step.

Alberta turned to look at the porter—now unmov-ing, statuary hands resting on the countertop. She said, "Speaking of which ... I believe that man ought to bathe. He's wearing enough aftershave to make a bear stop dead in its tracks. I'd guess that he's trying to cover up his ripe-ness. Maybe we should leave him a discreet note: 'Sir, it will be to the benefit of all that you wash yourself. Signed, A Concerned Passenger.' What do you think?"

"Well, no, Mother. Or, yes. No aftershave, I agree. But bathing? I think if we want to honour your vision and return to our prehistoric former glory, he should tear off his uniform and revel in his stink. We all should. Your mighty brontos didn't wear any trousers, did they?" His mother's visions were grand, Winston had seen, and fuzzy; she didn't care too much about details so long as it looked poetically just. Winston thought she'd regret yet that she'd raised a details man. It would be Alberta's enduring lament, the final word on her epitaph.

"Very well, you win. Read your damned book, then, young man." She was grumbling but already laying out framed cloth, thread, and needles—the tools for her embroidery. Winston was fond of his mother's pillowcase abstractions, which were always received with such expressions of puzzlement by the Women's Auxiliary. Of the donated helter-skelter chunks of livid silk and mossy wool thread, she'd say, "I call it 'Children on May Day'" (or "Washington Crossing the Delaware" or "Louis Riel at Batoche"), as though it was a perfect replica of a nostalgic Currier & Ives plate. The women, some decades younger than their benefactress, would politely encourage the senile biddy as though she had handed them a clod of earth and claimed it was brilliant 24-carat gold. Each time they carried in the selection of pillow covers, they'd chime, "Why, thank you, Mrs. Wilson, you've been so busy lately" with a nurse's pragmatic insincerity.

Winston believed his mother took no small pleasure from their smugness and discomfort, though she never said a word about it. While pretty French manor scenes stitched by other ladies seemed to be sitting on every chesterfield in town—the single setting of bewigged but chaste youthful romance on a swing had become the inexplicable staple of the River Bend City ladies' repertoire—Winston had never spotted one of Alberta's pillow covers in the house of any colleague or acquaintance. Their absolute invisibility led him to conclude that the women threw them out before they could scare the public during the Auxiliary's Christmas and Citizen's Day sales. We have a reputation for discerning taste to uphold, he supposed they might proclaim.

As she worked on a new extravaganza in buttercup yellow (maybe "Laura Secord on the Plains of Abraham"? She always chose a historical tableau), Winston could read. There was now scarcely enough time to finish the chapter. Winston was curious to know how the author was going to manage with the Minotaur legend. Already, as they had been speaking signs of human habitation had supplanted alder and salmonberry; boats and barges gave testimony about the economic value of a streaming body of water. Invective could replace Alberta's romance of brontosaurus paradise with lightning speed: majesty was covered with blight.... Winston knew what to expect.

🦆

Outside the station, they stood for the moment next to one of the fluted columns—tall and solid as a Douglas fir—and took in the hectic scene.

Alberta secured her hat and straightened her gloves. She looked at the sunny cut-glass chrysanthemum she'd pinned to her coat. "Is it a bit much?" she asked.

"No, Mother, it's perfect for the day."

"Should we walk there? It can't be far." Being outside her familiar routine had turned Alberta unusually ruffled, Winston noticed.

"Yes it can. Let's splurge, Mother. We'll catch a cab. You can close your eyes and reunite with your brontosaurus pals. We ought to wait over there, though." He walked toward a stand of taxicabs.

Following closely behind, she said, "Smart alec. Rouse me when we've arrived at our palace."

Winston had arranged the earliest possible appointment and fully expected to be out of the podiatrist's office in a matter of ten minutes. Greeting him with an automatic "Hello, Mr. Wilson. Lovely weather, isn't it?" the receptionist led the way to the same cramped examination room and reminded him to remove his shoes and stockings. Winston noticed the walls had been painted, lemon yellow over Kelly green, one coat only and not quite thick enough.

When the doctor arrived with his notebook in hand, he immediately bent on one knee and lifted Winston's foot. "Huh. I'll be darned," he exclaimed. He handled Winston's ankle and calf, pressing here and there to measure the swelling. Grinning now: "Huh. And that's my professional opinion, Mr. Wilson. My diagnoses have been about as helpful as your mother's mustard poultice. All I can say is that it's a mystery, but at least it's a harmless one. And as long as you're not too uncomfortable, you're going to have to get used to having a spongy foot and a tight shoe. I could lance it, I suppose," he muttered as he wrote in his notebook. He drew strong lines through *metaplasia.*

"Another six weeks, doctor?"

"No, I don't think so. If the swelling increases, book an appointment. Otherwise ... well, welcome to the future." He snapped the book shut and glanced at his wristwatch.

"It was a pleasure to make your acquaintance, Mr. Wilson." Grinning again, the doctor thrust out a fraternal hand. Winston wondered if he ought to smile with the same frequency; outwardly, the doctor's life-long success seemed assured.

Winston left feeling flustered, finding in his behaviour the very picture of the hypochondriac who believes that a tiny welt left by an insect was the seed for a blistering fever and terminal case of malaria. He'd always detested boys who cried wolf.

Winston bade the elderly elevator operator adieu with a tip of his hat and strode to the creamy-tiled Hudson's Bay outpost in under ten minutes. Seated in the vestibule of the south entrance as they'd arranged, Alberta gave him a discreet and queenly wave as she noticed him emerging from the chrome doors. "You're right on time, that was a fine guess," she said.

"You've found nothing to purchase, Mother?" She'd rested her boxy oxblood purse on her lap, but carried no shopping bags. Winston was struck by how contented she appeared.

"There's hardly been a minute to spend a cent. The perfume counter alone kept me busy, thank you very much, for half an hour. Those broads are cutthroat: 'No woman is complete without her secret weapon.' Were you aware of that? So I was informed. It reminded me of the poster that loomed over the post office for years: 'Tell Nobody—Not Even Her. Careless Talk Costs Lives.' Or some such tripe. You'd think we started wars, every one of us a plotting Mata Hari in the making. Huh! Still, I was nearly suckered into buying a small bottle."

Winston had taken a seat as his mother was relating her adventure. He said, "You ought to indulge yourself once in a while," and got up quickly to hold the door for a smartly dressed young woman overburdened with packages. "Maybe not all at once, though: a blind man might mistake you for a bouquet of carnations right now."

"Oh my. My sense of smell gave up the ghost five minutes after I arrived at the counter." She lifted her wrist to her nose. "It'll fade soon enough. Let's hope."

Now standing beside his mother's chair, Winston added: "You know, I think Mr. Carlyle actually kept that poster up for years after V-Day because Doris left him. He's such a bitter fellow. He'd refer to 'an ill wind' with a wink after a friendly lady left his wicket."

"Maybe he should have learned to drink a little less and keep his hands to himself, silly man. Everybody concerned would be happier." She had not nurtured many friendships, but Alberta managed to be up to date with grapevine dispatches. Returning home with staff room gossip, Winston was usually confounded that she'd heard details that hadn't passed his way.

Alberta told him that she was giddy as a bride, and had spent the hour wandering through several floors crawling with merchandise. The bins, shelves, and stacked towers of tinned goods in the Food Department made the Bend shops look like chicken scratch, as if they were still living in the Depression, she exclaimed. And the prices weren't bad, either.

"There's enough to clothe an army. We can wander through it all later," Alberta added. "You must be hungry, though. Any good news from the specialist?"

She was up and moving before he answered. Wandering along the aisle, she explained that she'd made a reservation for luncheon at the Marine Room, a fancy restaurant she had happened across on the top floor. "It's a lovely room. I requested that our table overlook the water. The hostess said she thought there would be something available. We'd best not be late."

Winston was hungry and, now, curious. He asked, "You're sure? We're not far from rail tracks here, Mother, we could head that way for a thriftier meal. We could split a can of pork and beans with some tramps down that way. Shoot some dice for dessert. I'd guarantee the view would be great there, too."

"Yes, I suppose we could. But...." She slowed for a moment to caress a diaphanous sun-coloured scarf worn by a blank-eyed plaster head. "You have plenty of money squirreled away, and you're buying. All the ladies will be impressed: A Good Son Taking His Delicate Mother Out For Luncheon." Her left hand semaphored the words in capital letters. "They'll all have the same thought, I can promise you that."

Alberta led him to a marble-clad wall punctuated with three bronze elevators. Riding the middle car, they remained silent till arriving at the sixth floor. Together or alone, they felt uncomfortable holding conversations at spots where they were sure of being overheard; in bank and post office lineups or the grocery store check-out, their concern was with getting through before being trapped by a chatty Mrs. Bell or Mr. Jenkins into shooting the breeze about the weather, the price of stamps or the latest setback on the new bridge. That compulsion of men to speak—to say just anything at all to halt the birth of silence—was one they did not share.

The elevator panel's square button lit **6** and a bell dinged their arrival. Stepping quickly out of the car Alberta said, "This way, sir," with mock-solemnity and mimicked the white-gloved military hand directions of a policeman at a busy intersection. Winston followed her signs.

En route to the Marine Room, they passed under a long and narrow showcase corridor. Winston studied its vaulted stained glass ceiling. The patriotic scenes of British Columbian industriousness had been captured with chunky leaded rectangles and translucent glass, a year of cutting and soldering at least, he guessed. Such an undertaking! An undulating indigo banner proclaiming *A Century of Progress* in bright yellow ran through the centre, and on either side were illustrated the provincial hallmarks as deigned by some centennial committee—**Energy and Power, Recreation, Fisheries, Forestry and Logging, Mining, Agriculture, Education, Commerce.** Winston noted that **Education** was represented by a milky one-room schoolhouse that looked forlorn and minute on what must be a wheat field surrounded by intimidating panes of deep green Emily Carr forest. Not quite the picture of today, he thought, but accurate enough. Then as now, **Agriculture** and **Forestry and Logging** were the careers of choice for many of the future breadwinners attending River Bend High. He noticed that there was no panel dedicated to Arts and Culture. A Century of Progress indeed.

Winston was impressed, even if he would have changed two or three of the highlighted provincial hallmarks. The Bend's puny Centennial stab was another story altogether. Beside throwing in some half-baked special events for the 1958 Citizen's Day parade—the mayor and his deputy dressed as the town's two founding missionaries and a dozen frisky aldermen dressed as Indian chiefs, railway men, coolies, and lady entertainers; and the high school's entire marching band decked out as Atomic Age strawberries following two straw-hatted farmers holding a **Land of the Big Red Strawberry** banner—the town's biggest effort had been renaming the new concrete bridge in honour of the province's Century of Progress. Centennial Bridge: what lyricism. Compared to this graceful lighted canopy, that centennial enterprise was an embarrassing cache of fool's gold.

Alberta had already seen this outpouring of provincial pride, or was not interested. Abandoning her traffic cop routine as they passed through, she was thinking aloud, casting herself as a career girl in a fantasy of city dwelling. "I wonder if I could get a job here, become an elevator lady. You think they'd hire me, or am I already too much of a relic?" she asked.

Winston surged with affection and took his mother by the arm. "Too old? You? I'm sure they'd take you on. You're a natural. You could offer perfume samples too. Tell the women they are incomplete unless they purchase the secret weapon now in your possession and available to them for mere pennies. You'd be a manager in no time." His tone was jocular even though he was sincere.

"You think? It'd be an adventure, at least a part-time one." She was swinging her purse as they came to the end of the corridor.

"Here we are," Alberta said at the heavy cedar doors, carved, Winston saw, with scenes borrowed from the glass ceiling. He thought to ask whether the department store had entered and won a competition during centennial. Alberta strode toward the hostess, a pale unsmiling matron with tight swirls of black braided hair. The woman turned to indicate a table by the window that was being set for them by a pair of girls wearing lacy white aprons over top stiff aqua pinafores.

"Stern Mrs. Danvers over there says we'll have our panoramic view in two minutes," she reported with an elated grin.

She took a few steps past the hostess's post, absorbed by the watery expanse just beyond the window. Winston studied the room, his attention first drawn to the lit tapers in trident candelabras sitting at opposite ends of the skirted banquet table. Barely visible, their light served no purpose in such a bright room except decoration, he decided. Between them lay the platters of elaborate food—rolled, wrapped, knotted, stuffed, or else spiked with toothpicks—that formed the room's centrepiece. Outside that inner circle sat jellied salads, coleslaw, smoked salmon, devilled eggs, celery stalks, rolls and biscuits, olives, pickles, condiments. At the far end: a deep metal tray heated with a kerosene flame that he guessed held scalloped potatoes and a layered chicken casserole. A smaller circular table promised them puddings, pies, and cakes garlanded with pastel icing.

Except for the chef carving bite-sized slivers of ham, turkey, and roast beef, Winston was the only man present. He saw that all the women had dressed up, some not removing their gloves until their orders had been taken. The bare arms and exposed backs, though, was a Marine Room fashion he could predict would not be catching on in the Bend. Farmers and loggers might admire that sort of thing in burlesque dancers they'd sneak out to gawk at across the river in Clear Brook, but never on their wives—who were expected to churn out the children while remaining as prim as nuns.

The hostess walked to the table and placed menus at each of their settings. There would be a waitress to serve them presently, she explained.

"She's seen this all hundreds of times before," Alberta said once the woman had returned to her station.

Winston smiled, sure that if the window could open, his mother's head would be stuck out of it, catching the rush of sea air.

"It's strange to think one could get tired of something so spectacular."

"Well, Mother, even you change teas from season to season." Winston was staring outside, focused on nothing in particular, wondering if sailors ever suffered from a marine sort of snow blindness.

"That's different," she replied.

They pored over the menu for a moment before deciding on the buffet.

In the spirit of fun, Alberta ordered a Jolly Fishwife. Winston read that it contained rum, grenadine, and pineapple juice, but imagined that an actual fishwife—an improbable mythical creature like a farmer's daughter, he thought, the butt of jokes men tell in beer parlours after they've had a few—was likely to drink straight from the bottle. Who could blame her? He told the waitress—younger and fairer than the hostess yet no less frosty—that he would be satisfied with water alone. She pointed to the plates available next to the chef.

"Heavenly days," Alberta exclaimed at the banquet table. "What a selection." She chose samples of everything, and even questioned the chef about turkey stuffing that was nowhere to be seen. She spoke her mind: "You can't have one without the other. I'd like a smidgen if you can dig some up." Winston's choices were fastidious: no olives, nothing with mayonnaise in it, no salmon.

Throughout the meal, their conversation was the usual merging of flows and eddies. They imagined the view as it was now and as it might have been in Alberta's Age of the Dinosaurs. With a smirk, Alberta added "doctor" to her list of career possibilities after Winston told her about the specialist's timid brand of diagnosis. Winston presented his mother with a short list of possible activities for the remainder of the day, but she waved aside the list and said she would like to walk through a park planted head to toe with flowers. The so-called park in the Bend was a memorial for the Great War circled by overgrown and unkempt greenery.

Over the years, Alberta had sent numerous letters to the city council about it—polite ones filled with practical and thrifty suggestions at first, then a wheedling pair, and finally a terse note whose lines veered toward vitriol. Aged and infirm veterans sat there gathering wool and speaking of *fighting the good fight* amongst themselves and to passersby, while younger layabouts and their rough-mannered girls smoked cigarettes and treated them with a palpable contempt tempered with false civility. A patch of dusty, butt-strewn petunias looking parched and dissipated in summer was as florid as it ever got.

They decided on a huge blossomy rectangle of a park in the city's southern reaches, agreeing it would likely be nearly overrun with flowering Dutch bulbs. Winston guessed that its splendor might reawaken his mother's reformist spirit and produce a fresh batch of splenetic letters.

Winston looked at his mother and felt happy that she was taking such pleasure with the day. Alberta's routine was so entwined with his and she'd been Mother for so long that he overlooked that she might have ambitions other than household cleanliness, gardening, and making them meals three times a day. A career, unlikely as that was, could be one of them. Why not move to the city and become an elevator woman at the Hudson's Bay Company? She might even marry. Who could say? His inviting her along had turned out to be a benefit for them both.

They finished with coffee—served in bone china, no less—and samplings from the dessert table. Winston told his mother that the Marine Room custard was nowhere close to hers. Looking forward to taking him through the highlights of the department store and getting across the city to view flowering trees and beds of blossoms, Alberta recommended they pick up the pace. Winston waved to their waitress.

As they stood and readied themselves for the afternoon, Alberta said, "Alright then, sir, let me show you around." She resumed her policing act, white gloves beckoning him now toward the elevator. He smiled, thinking how infectious her enthusiasm had become.

On the main floor at long last, Alberta and Winston planned their route to Queen Elizabeth Park from downtown. Winston agreed to their taking a bus, and refrained from suggesting an easy and quick taxicab.

"Before we move another muscle, though, I'm off to the Ladies' Room." Alberta handed her two shopping bags to her son.

"I'll wait right here," he said.

He was testing his eyesight—one eye squeezed shut, the other discerning shapes on the distant banks of shoes— when a voice interrupted him: "Excuse me, sir, we're running a special offer in the Men's Department. Today only!"

The voice was unmistakable. Winston turned and said, "Well, hello, Dickie. What a surprise. You're walking around the store advertising your department?" In a grey suit and somber striped tie, hair combed and parted neatly on the right, Dickie was the picture of an up and coming store clerk.

"No, you dizzy thing, that was for your ears only. I'm running an errand for Management, in fact." He raised his brow and tilted his head to indicate some documents in his hand. As always, his tone implied that there was trouble lurking below the calm surface: classified information, for instance, that could fall into the wrong hands.

Department store secrets, Winston thought, imagining spies from Woodward's infiltrating unlit rooms in the dead of night, flashlights in hand, sussing out enemy plans secured within filing cabinets. It seemed ludicrous, but who knew? Even he had been transfixed by the Rosenberg case—not least because the pair looked so innocuous. Their double-dealings remained a mainstay of conversation at work and at home for months. A lament had been uttered by practically everyone: If you couldn't trust your neighbours, then what was left to believe in?

The War and the tensions that had risen since then had made folks suspicious, Alberta complained now and then. "It's hardly necessary. I mean, why in God's name would any enemy power be interested in a sleepy valley in Canada?" she'd asked him one afternoon. Having gotten caught in a tangle of conversation—the proposed setting up of sentinels at the bridge and western exit of the city to alert citizens about the arrival of Soviets was a topic that had town lips flapping—at the Post Office, she was exasperated and in need of a kindred spirit. "Unless there's a strategic importance to strawberries and lumber the government hasn't told us about. Maybe they can make rocket fuel out of them." The idea was so risible they'd both laughed and coughed up their tea. While they had poked fun at the possibility of local clandestine lives and cloak-and-dagger goings-on, they could not help holding a few newborn reservations, or think of truths disguised by appearances: who could say?

Dickie took a step closer to Winston and glanced around before explaining, "You see, I'm hoping to move up the ladder. Before long I'm going to have a secretary who will take dictation. Just a matter of patience and timing, that's what Johnny says. Then I'll be heading out for three-martini lunches at the Empire Club. Just you wait and see."

As before, Winston felt himself at a loss for words. He drew back from Dickie and remained silent.

Dickie continued: "And you? You just happened to take a vacation from Mudville and happened to be shopping at the Hudson's Bay, I suppose. It tickles me that you wanted to stop by here. What a friendly gesture."

Winston had not forgotten about Dickie's love affair

with himself. "It's a surprise running into you, but in fact we are shopping here. Mother and I. We ate lunch in the Marine Room and have been touring the floors. That's why I'm here."

"The salt of the earth mother? Here? I'm seeing something primordial." Dickie surveyed the vicinity like an African safari hunter who is anticipating some ghastly creature slithering toward unsuspecting innocents. Dickie's feverish imagining was funny, but Winston realized he drew blanks when he tried to guess what such a thing would look like.

After no more than a beat, Dickie exclaimed: "I simply must run, though, gotta grab the brass ring. 'Those who hesitate are lost' and all that gung-ho management bunkum. Say, we are grabbing a bite tonight in Chinatown at the Bamboo Terrace. It's our haunt *du jour*. The chicken chow mein's divine and the mezzanine's better yet. We'll probably head over to the ol' Port-Land for a glass or three afterward. Say about seven give or take fifteen minutes. Care to partake?" He adjusted his tie's perfect knot.

"Thank you, Dickie. I'll keep that in mind."

"Ta-ta," Dickie said before moving onward to Management at a motivated pace. Dickie looked back. Winston waved in reply to the smile of his acquaintance.

Alberta returned just as Winston resumed his eye self-examination. "Who was that clerk talking to you?" she asked. "I figured he was selling something so I watched his pitch from over there." She thumbed over her right shoulder.

"No, I don't think he was selling me anything, Mother.

Remember when I told you about the odd fellow I met last time I was in the city? The one who took me to a seedy beer parlour? That was him. Dickie."

"I see. I was thinking I'd not likely buy something from him. A bit of a flaky pastry, looked like to me. Shifty." Alberta's mistrust of salesmen was boundless.

"The jury's still out about him as far as I'm concerned," Winston said, and quickly added: "But we really ought to get a move on, Mother. We don't want to be viewing flowers in the twilight." He'd prefer to guard Dickie from Alberta's feline curiosity.

"Southward ho, then. You mind carrying the bags still?" She strode toward the exit.

On the bustling streets outside the department store block, they walked toward the bus stop. A pretty girl at the perfume counter had sketched them a map after Alberta purchased a delicate ampoule of Empress Jean from her. Winston thought they'd need to refer to it often, so his mother kept it clutched in her hand. Before passing the city's first jail and courthouse—the imposing planes of grey stone evidently fertile ground for moss patches and streaks of slime—they paused at a rectangular cinder block pile set atop plywood on an adjacent lawn. Jade green letters on un-painted wood explained the crude shed:

### Junior Chamber of Commerce
### Cement Fallout Shelter

The sign on its roof inspired Winston's vision of cheerful high school Honour Roll students banding together to build protection from atomic bomb fallout with the same pep they might muster for decorating a themed holiday social or graduation dance.

Alberta frowned and said, "Doesn't look like it would withstand a strong gust of wind," then strode toward the door-less entrance.

"I suppose it would be underground, Mother, not just sitting there on somebody's front lawn," Winston replied.

Winston could not say for sure. He remembered that Cameron McKay had touched on the topic during one of his staff room harangues. Was it that a shelter had to be at least ten feet below the surface or that they must spend ten days underground before it was once again safe to creep back outside into the light? Winston clearly recalled that the chemistry teacher had claimed that *people would fry*—the image of sputtering bacon in a cast iron skillet had instantly leapt up in his mind—but was hazy about the details.

He'd never spent many minutes worrying about it. The Bend was so far away from any place that might look tempting to those Fate-like bomber pilots speeding through the heavens: why waste effort on flat farmland? Even the school's Safety Committee—student welfare watchdogs Delilah Pierce and Cameron McKay had combined forces at the tail end of the Korean War and no one had joined up since—had deemed atomic bomb drills unnecessary. The pair would meet at the beginning of each school year and then immediately afterward offer their assessment in the staff room, always closing with a proviso: "Pending political developments." Winston believed their caution was actually paranoia.

A pretty young blonde woman approached them just after Alberta stepped outside the shelter. She smiled and bade them "Good afternoon." As she handed a pamphlet to Alberta, Winston noticed her gloves were coloured a rosy pink. The blonde said, "It's going to be the death of all," and moved toward another clutch of pedestrians. There was no anger or hysteria in her voice; her forget-me-not eyes suggested calmness and focus. She seemed matter-of-fact, her certainty unruffled—as though she had just studied the approaching clouds and her years of expertise had let her determine with unquestionable authority that rain would fall any minute. All of her faculties were intact, clearly.

Like the Jehovah's Witnesses with their end of the world proclamations who used to visit Wilson Manor—Alberta had shooed them away rudely enough that they had apparently decided that the Wilsons were beyond salvation—this young lady had permanently made up her mind about a singular idea. No amount of evidence to the contrary would seep into her peculiar awareness of the world. Winston granted that she had greater cause for worry than those door-to-door evangelists with their predictions of the imminent arrival of the Four Horsemen that once uttered were then regularly revised. Even so, it was possible to err too far on the side of caution. The poor girl might end up like a mole living in a windowless basement.

"Well," Alberta exclaimed, and showed him the folded paper. Its message was deadpan, as though typed by a dour scientist: indisputable data for the reader to consider—

> You live in a target area.
> You must get beyond this 20 mile
> limit to be reasonably safe.

A long list of related facts filled the sheet. An address had been printed on the back. Readers were implored to contact their local political leaders. Winston could not imagine what one would say should he decide to write a letter. The likelihood of any local politician getting riled up about the threat of nuclear bombs looked remote: what could he hope to accomplish, after all? The matter would be out of his league.

"Now there's a fine reason not to take that job at the Hudson's Bay," Alberta remarked. "Unless of course Bailey's Farm is also a target. Those damned strawberries. Then we'll be done for." She slipped the pamphlet into her purse and turned her attention to the girl's crude map and waved it at him. "Flowers will cure what ails us, my dear," she said warmly.

The street was radiant and festive, lit by a strand of pulsating colours, each one amplified by the fresh slick of rain on cars and pavement and put into stark relief by the starless night sky. Next to the flashing gold, red, and blue of Ming's FAMOUS CHINESE FOODS, the cool green neon leaves and glaring yellow stalks of *Bamboo Terrace* Fine Chinese Food formed an inviting arbor. Winston decided the restaurant's striped metal awning, the only one he had noticed in the entire area, was an incongruous but pleasantly homey touch.

At the Hudson's Bay, Dickie had not been specific about details, and Winston was already worried that he had no idea whether a reservation had been made, if one could be made, and whose name it would be under. Making a fool of himself: that was what he strived to avoid. Seeing his own inclination to worry about details stir to motion, he told himself not to get flustered. It was a bantam-sized restaurant so they would probably be seated in plain sight. The moment he stepped inside, they'd beckon him. He wondered if his on-the-dot punctuality would cause him grief. These men struck him as being slapdash about a social nicety like timeliness.

Through double doors—solid glass and heavy as lead—Winston was still for a minute as his eyes responded to the assault of fluorescence. Like the Port-Land, this place was no different from others he'd visited. The Bend's Prawn Gardens, where he and Alberta had eaten beef chop suey too many times to count, was a carbon copy—a coat of paint a mint lozenge hue that was decorated with lanterns and misty watercolour nature scenes glued onto rectangles of splintered bamboo; particles of scent—onion, fish, soy sauce—hung heavily in the humid air. This slight variation boasted two plaster statues of Oriental ladies in flowing robes, one at the cash register and the other at his feet. It was cookie cutter otherwise. And lit so brightly it could substitute as a surgery theatre. Winston noticed that all the tables were packed with Oriental families. Now, that was definitely not the case anywhere in the Bend.

There was no sign of Dickie. Maybe the gang had changed its dinner plans. At the far right, Winston saw a narrow staircase and grinned in relief. He pointed to it when an elderly woman with unnaturally jet hair approached. Gauging by her silky emerald dress, Winston concluded she must be the hostess. Yet she remained impassive, speaking no words and giving no welcoming gesture. While Winston couldn't see the gang, he did recall Dickie's comment about the mezzanine. When the hostess maintained her ghostly silence—Winston imagined she was trying to intimidate him so that he'd leave—he stepped past her toward the stairs. Hoping to avoid any awkwardness with the mute hostess, he did not turn around to see her response. He felt foolish pushing past her, but bolting out the door would have been worse.

Winston looked up to see that a worn carpet runner began at the midpoint of the wooden stairs. Ahead, the light was faint; he fancied that he was about to enter an opium den and smiled at his unfounded expectations; if nothing else, the Port-Land had taught him that lesson. He reached the top and stood before a room of chattering Caucasian faces—unencumbered adults, their children at home with babysitters. Spotting the gang at a distant table, he noted that they had chartered a new member. Winston paused to take in the surroundings. The contrast between floors was startling; it looked as though a tornado had ripped one restaurant from its original location and slammed it atop another. If it was no decadent lair for dreamy, slack-muscled addicts with heavy lids, there was no denying its exotic lushness. The room ably met his oversized expectations.

The sight prompted a recollection of a production of *The Mikado* put on by the Valley Players he and Alberta had attended a few years back. Here, the walls were papered in muted golden brocade; narrow glass tanks holding darting fish and swaying aquatic plants divided the room. He saw that there were crabs, too, crowded at the bottom, their heavy claws knocking helplessly against the transparent wall of their prison. At the room's far end hung what appeared to be a caravan's wooden wheel thickly coated with red lacquer. Directly in front of it was a bronze Buddha—arms raised in celebration—on a platform of thick bamboo rods. The ceiling glowed green and blue; the lights were perched behind upturned paper umbrellas whose frames were visible like X-rayed bones. Regular beats of neon streetlight passed through the bare windows.

As he approached the table, he heard Dickie bark a demand: "Waiter, we need an extra chair."

With his back to the corner, Dickie had a clear vantage of the room. He spoke loudly: "Farmer, welcome aboard the SS *Shanghai*. We weren't sure you'd find your way. You'll have a chair in a sec. We ordered about half the menu, so there's plenty to go round."

Customers from other tables looked up. Winston flushed and wondered whether Dickie was already dead drunk. He glanced at his wristwatch.

A boy arrived just as Dickie finished his sentence. Winston imagined a hidden door that the waiters used instead of the narrow staircase.

"Thank you, Dickie."

"Left Mother to fend for herself, did you?"

"I couldn't be sure she'd enjoy herself."

"You think we're an acquired taste, do you?"

Winston smiled. Dickie's bantering game could be sabotaged by an unanswered question. "This place is fantastic." He turned to Johnny.

"Yes, it is, isn't it?" Johnny replied. "And while I'm able to get a word in edgewise.... Winston, you remember Ed, yes? This young man is Frankie, Frankie Jones, he's, er, my nephew."

"Nice to meet you, Frankie."

Frankie stood and extended his hand across the table. "Pleased to meet you, sir." Even in the kaleidoscopic lights, Winston could see that the cheeks of his pale marble face bloomed with a rose flush.

"Frankie here was in the army, so he's used to formality with 'senior officers.'" Dickie spoke with a master of ceremony's command.

Frankie shared his uncle's nervous caginess, though his crew cut and collegiate sweater made him appear less a wary gangster than a lanky, nail-biting student. Before sitting down, he handed a highball glass to Dickie.

As he glanced at each man, Winston realized that he was surprised and a touch disappointed that they were real. He had come to think of them as remote, having fantastic movie star lives that required constant costume changes and a stream of adventures. Yet here and now Winston could see that Ed's face could use a shave and that Dickie wore the same coat and tie, even though tonight he'd added a white carnation boutonniere. Their days had been running in routines similar to his since the last time they'd all been together. Work, chores, and leisure were constants; the difference was that their big city setting had deluxe venues.

"Would you like a drink? We're drinking Manhattans, so it's that or—blech!—jasmine tea." Dickie held up an empty glass.

"Is beer not a possibility?" Winston enjoyed the mixture of beer and salt. He and Alberta always shared a large bottle with their chop suey.

"Well, we didn't think to bring anything so proletarian."

In answer to Winston's perplexed face, Ed and Johnny—with competing Morse code bursts—explained that Chinatown merchants, like the Kwoks who owned Bamboo Terrace, had a longstanding feud with liquor control bureaucrats, and the result was often suspension of liquor licenses.

"They have philosophical differences," Dickie interjected.

Johnny, speaking on the side of laissez-faire Chinatown, favoured a lenient, pro-American stance ("This backwater province has its dainty little head stuck in the goddamned Prohibition. Everyone's a lot happier down south"), while Ed dizzily asserted that "rules are rules and everyone has to follow them," and that "rules are made to be bent."

Ed was good-natured, but not a man who would have said much of value on a high school debating team, Winston decided. The *happy medium* was the restaurant's mezzanine, where customers in the know could bring their own booze. It was a delicate arrangement: the proprietors were aware that Ed was a liquor inspector because his last official visit there had resulted in a letter that informed them of their suspended liquor license; they also counted on his bending the rules—if they looked the other way while the customers (including a provincial liquor inspector) defied an insignificant technicality of the law, then it would be a benefit to them the next time an official inspection passed by their address.

"It's rather Byzantine," Johnny said with a roll of his eyes. "Next thing you know we'll have some secret knock and handshake as though we belong to the Oddfellows. Temperance, how ridiculous. People should be free to do what they will." His testiness caused Winston to think he was personally affected by this arrangement. "Next time, Dickie, I say we drink Old Fashioneds. The shoe fits."

Winston wondered whether he had walked into the middle of a quarrel. While he could easily recall the men's banter, tonight their conversation was stained dark with anger. It was palpable. He'd seen siblings partake in bitter exchanges like this. He didn't feel he was close enough to them to ask who had offended whom.

"Well, then, Dickie, I'll have a Manhattan, thank you."

As Dickie poured from a thermos he stored near his chair, he said, "We prefer this cocktail wet, so I hope you don't mind your vermouth. And no maraschino cherry. Sorry, I'm not a lowly secretary, you know. At least it's chilled."

"That's fine, Dickie, you're such a dedicated host." Unlike Alberta, Winston had never developed a taste for hard liquor. Wet or dry, it was all Greek to him.

"Old-fashioned graft, hey?" Winston looked at Ed.

"Yes, Edwina, do tell. The whole table awaits your opinion," Dickie added, intensifying Ed's discomfort.

"Graft is a dirty word, criminals greasing the palms of politicians." He fidgeted with his pinkie ring as he spoke. "I think that 'Necessity is the mother of invention' has a truer ring to it. It's a better way to look at the situation, at least. There's a need, there's a goal, and there's an obstacle. The need pushes us to get around the obstacle in order to reach the goal so that we can be happier. So there. Practical."

"Very eloquently put, Ed. An on-the-spot allegory is not something just anyone can muster." Johnny spoke like an imperious chairman taken aback by a subordinate employee's solid report.

Ed turned his attention to his plate. Noting Johnny's misuse of *allegory*, Winston wondered how he'd react to being corrected. His wrath would be formidable. Winston was not prepared to meet it. In any form, Johnny's retort would be withering.

Ed turned his face from Winston to Johnny. He asked, "Are you being sarcastic? You know I can never tell with you."

A flock of waiters arrived carrying plates and platters of food. Dickie named the inventory of dishes as the headwaiter—several decades older than his assistants—silently placed them on the rotating core of the table. The intense savory steam reminded Winston that cocktails were no substitute for dinner.

"Our duck. We're missing our duck." Dickie spoke to the elderly waiter.

"No duck." The waiter began moving from their table.

"Yes, I know it's obviously not here. We ordered it, however, and would like to eat it. Preferably now while the rest's still piping hot." Dickie had raised his voice.

The elderly waiter turned to his assistant, a jet-haired newt of a boy who looked no older than ten.

"We're sorry, mister. The kitchen ran out of duck a couple minutes ago." He added, "That item will not appear on your bill," after the headwaiter sprayed him with Chinese words.

"Thank you, young man." Dickie saluted him with his highball glass.

"You're really missing out, Hayseed. The crispy Peking duck here is the best in town." Winston smiled at Dickie. He thought of the Port-Land and his sense of watching characters on the silver screen. Here, though, the décor and conversation conspired to make him acutely conscious of being on stage. The evening had not yet revealed whether he had been cast in a comedy, melodrama or tragedy.

"But there's plenty here, and it's all good." Ed seemed set on enjoyment.

"You're really pushing that 'every cloud has a silver lining' bit tonight, aren't you," Johnny said, picking up the

Prohibition strand of their argument. He spun the pork chow mein in Ed's direction.

"It's better than seeing only gloom and rain." Ed had poured a volcanic island of mushroom fried rice into the middle of his plate.

Dickie cleared his throat theatrically and asked, "Shall I serve?" He held the thermos in his hand, pivoting it slowly like an intent mesmerist.

Winston could see that Frankie did not share his uncle's gift for public speaking. When he was not shoveling in his food as though it were his last meal, his attention was directed toward a young woman at an adjacent table of coarse-looking career girls. Her white angora sweater—at least a size too small, Winston gauged—was all hills and valleys.

"And what do you think, young Franklin?" Dickie had followed Winston's eyes.

"I was thinking about doing some skiing, sir. It's 'Frankie,' please." Frankie faced Dickie reluctantly, his thick brow furrowing.

"So long as I am paying for your tickets, Frankie, you might want to pay attention to the gentlemen you're keeping company with." Johnny's tone was a perfect vehicle for his disappointment.

"Are you visiting your uncle, Frankie, or do you live in town?" Winston decided his goal tonight should align with Ed's; he hummed *you've got to accentuate the positive* quietly.

Sweet yet potent, the Manhattan was going straight to his head.

Frankie rapidly shifted his attention from Winston to Johnny, but did not answer.

Johnny said, "Oh, Frankie is deciding if he wants to settle here for a while. His folks sent him up from Los Angeles. They thought he was falling in with a bad crowd, so they shipped him off to the country so that he could gain some perspective. Country air and all that. Isn't that the case, young man?"

"That's it, sir." Frankie was rigid and attentive.

"The city is home to one of the best universities in the country." Winston adopted a paternal demeanour he reserved for those shy and intent students who sought him out for counselling with a surprising regularity. While he had never visited any university campus, he trusted what he'd heard.

"C'mon, Farmer, you can only dive so deep in a shallow lake," Dickie commented before Frankie could say a word.

"Well, I hope you are finding the city worth your while, Frankie." Winston kept a strict focus on Frankie. He did not approve of how Dickie treated the young man and wanted to smooth over the rough edges of the conversation.

"Yes, Frankie's become a regular nature lover, if his hikes through Lord Stanley's Park are anything to judge by. A real pro. He must have legs like Johnny Weissmuller."

"Dickie, please shut up," Johnny barked. "For Christ's sake. You just don't know when to quit, do you?" Dickie's face was set, an expressionless mask. He collected up the glasses from the table so that he could pour a fresh round of Manhattans. He lifted the thermos. "Oh-oh. It's empty. The party's over. Let's get home before we sober up," he said.

Winston's discomfort was escalating. He felt certain that a dispute was still running between the men, though he had missed its beginning. The expression about cutting tension with a knife was perfectly illustrated at their table. Winston had never exchanged hard words with Alberta. Even when they disagreed they never spoke harshly. He made up his mind: lifting that tension would be the most prudent tact he could take.

"Johnny, did you meet your nephew when you were in Hollywood?" It was a story Winston guessed that Johnny could not resist.

"Oh Lord, not that. I am going to use the facilities," Dickie said, leaving no doubt that anything would be preferable to being present as Johnny's tale unraveled. He stood up, carefully pushed his chair close to the table, and cut a fast track to the staircase.

"Yes, it was something like that, though it took us awhile to run into each other."

"I'd like to hear about it, if you don't mind."

"Well, why not?" Johnny raised his brows, suggesting that if anyone had any objections, now was the time to express them. Frankie and Ed concentrated on the remaining food.

"It was a bright lights, big city kind of deal. After being canned by Malkin's, Tinseltown seemed like the best bet. I had grand ambitions. I thought Hollywood would be the sort of place where a man could get off the train and walk to MGM Studios and take a job, and six months later he'd be making a movie, collaborating with Edith Head and trying to calm Bette Davis's frayed nerves with French champagne and cigarettes by the crate. Or vice versa. And, naturally, rolling in the dough. The thing is, everybody who goes there believes the same dream. It's the oldest story. But I didn't learn that until I'd already stepped right in."

"That's a terrific story, Johnny. Does anyone want more mushroom rice?" Ed was reaching for the platter. Winston patted his own belly for Ed's benefit.

"I haven't quite wrapped up the story, Ed, as you might have noticed if you were paying attention. So, anyway, Winston, it knocked me off my high horse, I'll tell ya. Nobody knew Malkin's, my agency, nothing. Hell, they wouldn't recognize goddamned Winnipeg if I gave them a souvenir box of Red River black flies. I did get work, though, that was a cinch. My first job was with the costume department at the Republic Pictures studio. That didn't work out." He added, *sotto voce*: "Here, if you get fired, it's bad news. There, well, it's as common as sunshine.

"Then I branched out. Tried acting, became an extra. I played up my PR skills and got on re-writing a program called *Honeychile*. I don't imagine you saw it? That was an experience, I tell you. The pace was something I could not get used to. One job, then another, and a whole new set of folks to work with. Not to mention mean, stingy personalities. And let's not say even a word about that desert climate. It was all too much. So I settled down, and slaved away in some rinky-dink public relations company that did studio business. I thought it would be a foot in the door."

"Pride goes before the fall," Ed commented, then asked Frankie to divide the remaining chow mein with him. Looking toward the staircase for Dickie, Winston could see that the mezzanine was emptying out.

"Anyway, one day I was in some Tiki dive on the Boulevard with a couple of cronies and who comes in but Vera Hruba Halston, dripping B glamour, a shade too much flash, looking trampier than Flame LaRue. Her gal pal is none other than Judy Canova. I'd worked with that hillbilly before and had met her on *WAC from Walla Walla*. Don't know if anyone sat through that gem." Johnny surveyed his audience. He lit a cigarette and placed the match on his plate.

As he approached the table, Dickie rolled his eyes. "We all saw it, I'm sure, Johnny. Everyone in this place." His gesture swept through the room. "I'm surprised no dreamy-eyed secretary has cornered you and begged for an autograph." Winston felt his face redden as adjoining tables noticed the commotion. In public and in large doses, Dickie's flamboyance became an embarrassment. Winston stood and pulled the chair out for Dickie. The patrons would lose interest once he was seated.

"All settled in, missy?" Johnny's voice was chilly, his words aiming to put Dickie in his place. "Okay then. Well, I didn't exactly work *with* Judy but on the same picture. As an extra. And they even gave me a line: 'Yes, sir.' I was a clerk in the army clerical pool. An unforgettable performance, I tell ya." Winston's lips stretched from the urge to laugh; if the sheer extravagance of their talk was shocking, it was also delectable. They had no shame, not caring a whit that they were drawing comments. What would those other customers be saying, he wondered.

"Did you see *I Was a Shoplifter*? Even Rock Hudson had to start somewhere," Dickie barked.

Ed said, "I saw that. Where was Rock?"

"It was just a bit part. He was an auto mechanic, I think. Now there's a career for young Franklin ... an auto mechanic, I mean, not a bit player."

"Are you sure? I remember the mechanic. It wasn't him, I'm sure of it." It was a mystery Ed needed to solve.

"It doesn't really matter, Edward, the point is that everyone, even the biggest star, has to start somewhere." For a second, Dickie was an effigy of exasperation, his pitch none other than that of a teacher with students who are slow to grasp a simple idea.

"Ladies, do you mind? I am trying to answer Winston's question, not gossip like a schoolgirl. Dickie, the well's really run dry?" Johnny held up his highball glass.

"Afraid so, my dear. Next time each of us will have to smuggle in a thermos."

"I hope Winston knows what we're going on about," Ed said to the gang.

Winston had heard all the names, but was enjoying Johnny's fish-out-of-water tale. He replied: "My mother's the one who follows the lives of stars, not I, I'm afraid."

Johnny resumed his vivid storytelling. "Vera was like

Esther Williams, only on ice; instead of America's Mermaid she was ... I dunno, she didn't really catch on the same way. 'Skated out of Czechoslovakia and into the hearts of America.' That was how the studio packaged her, anyway. An accent heavy as Russian bread. Big brown cow eyes and a bosom like she was Jayne Mansfield's cousin from the old country. Sharp as a tack, though.

"So there I was, a bit soused. The cocktails were giving me Dutch courage, you know, and I thought I'd walk over to them with a proposition." He emptied his cocktail glass. "I said before that when I went to Hollywood with dreams of the big time, I didn't know that everyone from Flin Flon to Florida tries their luck there with the same fairy tale lodged in their head. By this time, though, I had learned that every two-bit player has some scheme they want to sell to a producer or a studio. I had an idea, too, you see. But I'll be damned if I was going to pitch it by going up to these ladies and saying, 'Excuse me, miss, I have this vision that'll make us all millionaires.'" Johnny's imitation of an eager nobody dreamer was shaded with kindness and contempt.

"I walked past them on the way to the toilet and nodded briefly at the hillbilly. On the way back she greeted me with, 'Corporal Clerk. Am I right or what?' I smiled and said, 'Yes, ma'am,' in a corny hick accent. They invited me to share a cocktail with them, and I thought 'Why not?' We got along like gangbusters. They were pissed and brimming with complaint. Men and movies, bastards and bitches, basically. Judy wanted Chekhov and got corn pone. Vera exclaimed that she was not bloody Carmen Miranda on skates. She wanted *Gentlemen Prefer Blondes*, she said, and got foreign temptress bits. Or was asked to skate. Or both…"—"Once you're typecast, it's curtains for your career," interjected Dickie with a slow knowing nod—"…and besides, as she said, she wasn't 'no spring chicken no more.' That woman had more cuss-words up her sleeve than a sailor."

The old waiter and his slip of an assistant appeared, clearing the table without a word. The boy returned with a scallop shell plate holding a bill and five fortune cookies. He asked if they wanted jasmine tea.

"We'll pass on the tea, young man. But thank you." Dickie gave the boy a grandfatherly smile. "God, who can drink that stuff? I'd rather sip gasoline," he said a beat later.

"So, I thought now would be as good a time as any to pitch my idea. Like some circus barker I said, 'Ladies, what do Laraine Day, Peggy Wood, Sally Rand, Una Merkel, Ilona Massey, Leatrice Joy, Pola Negri, Lola Lane, Blanche Yurka, and that lover of women Lizabeth Scott have in common?'" Johnny paused.

"They all know the same Mexican surgeon?" said Dickie, approximating Vera Hruba Halston's accent.

"Why, I can't say. They've had their day in the sun?'" said Ed with a Southern drawl.

Johnny smiled at their efforts. "I said, 'It's true they're all a bit older than twenty-five. But does their age make them box office poison? Nags that ought to be sent to the glue factory? Or does it make them veteran professionals with more tricks up their sleeves than a grifter?' Then I threw them my pitch, a talent agency"—Johnny drew a line with his index finger—"as yet unnamed that would represent a powerful corps of actresses, women who are usually considered used goods and who have no leverage with the studios because they're old news and has-beens. It was brilliant. And they agreed."

"And then you met your nephew that day," Winston asked. He remembered that it was to Frankie that the story was supposed to lead.

"Oh. Sorry, I got tangled up with the story of my life. Selfish me. I met Frankie at some party—there are a lot of parties, I tell you, those folks know how to live large. This particular one was put on by some producer celebrating his soon-to-be-released swords and sandals epic. The waitresses were dressed in costumes—Roman slave girls tailored in Vegas—and the bartenders and waiters were gladiators. Bronze-coloured Frankie was one of these Hollywood Romans." He smiled at his ward. "We talked a bit because I thought he looked familiar. And sure enough, he was."

"Phew, that's over with. Mr. Schmidt has been under the spotlight for days, he must be drenched. Are you certain you've gotten the whole story now, Farmer—fanciful as it is?" Winston watched the antagonists exchange glances.

"I'm sure of it, Dickie. Though I meant to ask about Pierre a while ago."

"Oh yes. La Contessa was feeling blue and decided to cloister herself with Dinah Washington for the evening."

"It's my turn to take care of the bill, gentlemen, so grab your fortune cookie." Johnny placed bills on the scallop. "Let's get out of this dump."

Winston felt caught up by Johnny's generosity. When he went out with school colleagues, they always divided up the bill exactly. "May I pay for my portion?" he said stiffly.

"Don't worry about it, Winston," Johnny said.

"That's generous of you, Johnny."

Johnny gave him a wink. "Besides, if you're back here often enough, your turn to pay will come up in no time at all. You'd better start socking away money now! Ed eats like a horse." They looked to Ed. He did not respond.

"Evening, ladies," Johnny tipped his hat at the nearest table. The woman with the white sweater waved exuberantly at Frankie. "Someone's going to have a bun in the oven in no time," Dickie whispered loudly to Ed.

Downstairs, the clatter of the restaurant had died down; the main floor was deserted except for the table where the waiters were playing a game with cards and ivory and red disks. Johnny asked the emerald-clad hostess to call a cab. She walked toward the kitchen without speaking a word.

"Is she always so quiet?" Winston asked the men.

Dickie answered in a beat: "The Empress? Yes, rumour has it that she's not said a single word since her husband took up with a white woman. Shame is a powerful force to these people."

"Shame has its place," Ed said.

"Say, we're going to head to my place to fortify ourselves with some cocktails. Dare to come along?" Winston wondered why Dickie's voice was so full of mischief.

"I'd best be getting back to the hotel. Mother will wonder what happened if I don't rise with her and the roosters at daybreak tomorrow. Thank you for the offer, though, Dickie." He gestured toward his hotel. "I think I'll just walk back the way I came." His voice felt constricted.

Winston felt he'd had enough conversation for the night. Groups—societies under glass with their own peculiar requirements and hidden rules—made him feel apprehensive, as much a fish out of water as Johnny in Tinseltown. And there were always judgments, too, swift and permanent. He recalled the boys who'd asked him to join their gang when he was in primary school. After telling Alberta about it, he'd reported back to the boys that his mother said they were trouble. It was a mistake—getting ahead meant tailoring the truth: hardly a fact a bookish child would intuit. The boys had retaliated by calling him a momma's boy. That spontaneously generated reputation had chased him now and again throughout high school. He'd obviously made the wrong choice, but had never imagined its repercussion. Now, naturally, he had seen that life was stockpiled with similar lessons—once learned, never forgotten—and thought that his knowledge was cold comfort indeed.

Winston pictured this new gang staying up late into the night—mixing drinks, squabbling, gossiping, and listening to music—and then leaving for work in wrinkled clothing without having slept a wink. He'd never done so himself. It seemed wrong to him even if he couldn't say precisely why. After all, he pondered as they bantered amongst themselves, we're not chickens that automatically fall to sleep as soon as the daylight fades. But standards and rules are here for a reason. His prim reaction to their supposed devil-may-care plans sounded like a lecture he might hear Miss Mittchel give one of her wisecracking back-of-the-classroom students. That naysayer's sanctimoniousness was no characteristic in himself he'd care to fertilize any further.

Outside, the men stood in the crackling neon bamboo grove and waited for their taxicab. The hard rain had mellowed to drizzle. Winston admired the play between the parti-coloured neon flashes and the rain slick cars and streets. It reminded him of the midways at home that delighted adults and children alike when they blazed into garish blossom.

"Neon light is very cheap, that's why all these businesses leave theirs running for so many hours," Ed explained, filling the lull. "I don't know why it buzzes like that, though."

"Don't feel that you have to wait for us, Winston," Johnny said. "You're hoofing it, not us."

"Yes, I'll be heading off, then, gentlemen. It was nice to see you all again. And a pleasure to meet you, Frankie." The young man stood unsmiling, legs rigid, his arms crossing his chest. Winston reached out to shake his hand.

"Sir." It was the sole word Frankie had uttered since being chastised. His sulking softened his military stance.

Passing by another neon-lit restaurant, Winston turned to wave. The last man on the street, Ed was now stepping into the black taxi. He shut the door and their vehicle shot into the night. As Winston walked in search of the spinning **W** to the west, his mother's interest in Dickie sprang to mind. She'd adore that restaurant and its secretive Prohibition-era atmosphere; she'd be only too happy to smuggle in a flask or two in her purse. As for the gang, he felt protective. He'd lessen their outlandishness—lock it in a compartment for himself only—when they chatted over breakfast about his banquet of Chinese delicacies.

🦢

No soul could doubt that the plump and tiny strawberry was the day's honoured guest. Its delectable shape could be seen everywhere—teeming in baskets, rendered and then sealed with wax in jars, floating with ice chunks in punch, transformed into costumes, cut out from painted wood and affixed to streetlights.

Winston and Alberta were watching a group of young crooners from the Women's Auxiliary perform a medley of songs sure to make a grandmother's eyes glisten with nostalgia. Their demure white dresses were set off by green string bracelets that sprouted dangling cloth berries. The singers had strolled onstage close on the felt-clad heels of the Valley Players, whose contribution to the day had been the rousing final act of the little known Shakespearean tragedy, *Strawmlet*. Scampering about during the parade, the Players had promoted themselves—a miracle of self-improvement—as the world's first strawberries performing in an Elizabethan drama. The audience had hooted and shouted good-natured insults when the red, man-sized Polonius came on stage; once the swordplay began, though, everyone in the crowd grew silent and watchful.

As they feinted back and forth, Winston studied the Players' backdrop. Painted who knows when and touched up over the years, the wooden wall depicted a berry farmer's paradise: the fantastically verdant and fertile Valley overflowing with strawberry fields. Granite mountains had metamorphosed into giant strawberry mounds capped by creamy peaks; a grand rainbow arced from one side of the valley to the other, all the while fighting the laws of nature, composed as it was from scads of the celebrated red marvels.

The mural was set up year after year and its fanciful vision never failed to elicit comment. Today, Alberta had wondered aloud about how badly the trots would course through the citizenry of that fairy tale kingdom. When they had bumped into Doc Carter, she'd asked for his professional opinion about a diet composed of nothing other than strawberries.

"You wouldn't get scurvy, that much is for sure," he'd smiled, "but the lack of red meat would have you as weak as a lamb in no time."

Strawberries abounded, but it was the spectacular weather that was common currency. June was fickle: every man was aware that a furious downpour was as likely as not. Tents and tarpaulins were ready and available, and gave no one satisfaction. It would be better to head home than crowd together dripping wet and irritable in a dank tent. Yet at noon no hint of clouds near or far gave pause for an anxious thought. It was neither scorching nor wet, and proclamations about the fineness of the day stood ready on the tips of myriad tongues.

Loud applause and a few shrill whistle bursts followed

the lament of stoic Fortinbras over the dead berries now strewn on the stage floor. After the Players bowed, the master of ceremonies—wearing a flower-garlanded top hat and a tuxedo coat with tails—wandered out to announce that a band of fiddlers would be setting up soon. His words gave the audience impetus to mill about.

"It's a grand day for the Strawberry Citizen's Derby, isn't it?" Alberta was peering westward into the sky.

Doc Carter nodded. "Couldn't ask for anything better."

"I thought of the 'Citizen's Strawberry Festival Soap Box Derby Day' while brewing my tea this morning. What do you think?"

"It's a bit of a mouthful. I'd vote for choosing just one. In a pinch, Citizen's Day would be my pick." Carter took off his sunglasses and shielded his eyes as he spoke.

"I'd choose it as well, though I have heard Cameron McKay say that he believes it smells of communism." Winston had already heard Alberta's idea; they'd invented ludicrous names for the day as they walked toward their customary vantage point in front of Klein's Delicatessen on 1st Avenue.

"Yes, well, he sees Russian infiltrators as often as I see sore throats." He cleared his throat and rolled his eyes.

Winston thought that the Bend's social calendar was becoming positively Roman with its summer celebrations. The miscellany of holidays was unprecedented. In the staff room, Winston had overheard some claim the festivity was simply an outpouring of euphoria, patriotism that had naturally bloomed in response to the losses and upsets of the War. Others—Cameron McKay vociferous among them—hinted darkly that it was actually a tiny, desperate finger in a dyke holding back the flood of economic decline; everyone in town lamented that the flats and hills on the south side of the river had long surpassed the Bend's berry output. Bend farms had never really recovered from the disastrous flood of '48, and the Japanese, who ran so many of the successful berry patches, took their enviable farming secrets with them when the government relocated them to the hinterlands following Pearl Harbor.

Lately, the Soap Box Derby had eclipsed the Strawberry Festival. It attracted zealous parent-chaperoned contestants from near and far; tourists loaded with cameras came all the way from Portland, Spokane, and Coeur d'Alene. The *Record* claimed it was a bonanza for business. Winston thought the true nature of the festival would sort itself out soon enough. More and more, though, strawberries did seem to belong in the past.

The derby finale—coming after countless heats and rounds that Alberta and Winston were not fervent enough to watch—was the cap of the day, announced with a gun shot at four p.m. after all the musicians and performers had completed their programs on the downtown stage. They grumbled about the derby and routinely vowed to take their leave after the entertainment on 1st Avenue. There was simply nothing to the sport ("It's no better than watching a tire roll down a hill" was Alberta's refrain) and once the final race ended—it took about one minute from hilltop to finish line—the imposing crowd jostled and pushed in its eagerness to return home. The Wilsons preferred the look of the day a few years back: the Strawberry Pageant and its crowning of the Festival Queen had been the day's big draw, followed in the evening by the Strawberry Social. Auctions, contests, stage performances, and the Strawberry Dunk had come in between.

Their taste was passing out of date, and they acknowledged it as being a whiff of nostalgia. The editor of the *Record*—a blowhard of a man fond of forecasting the rosy future of the Bend—had called for the Derby celebration to be spread out over an entire weekend. It was difficult to organize all the volunteers for a single day, he opined, and three days would also mean a greater volume of business. There was no shortage of outsiders, it would seem, who would travel for hours to the Bend to watch boys steer rocket-shaped vehicles down a moderately steep hill. Winston was of the opinion that the craze for boys in dinky racecars would fade as well. By contrast, Citizen's Day would last as long as the Bend possessed citizenry.

Now as always, the loud, spangled parade inaugurated the Day's festivities. Subdued in comparison to last year's centennial parade, it was again led by the mayor, who sat cross-legged on the hood of his Ford while his wife sat behind the steering wheel and waved. Close behind them marched the high school's band, playing their usual handful of tunes that included the *Viennese Waltz, Blue Moon Over Kentucky*, and snatches of the national anthem. The lithe players on the River Bend City Sikhs volleyball team walked steadily—keeping one gleaming white ball aloft—and on the occasion of their coach blasting his whistle the men broke into patterned steps as complicated as quadrilles; six men on the Flood Prevention and Emergency Committee frolicked with inner tubes wrapped around their waists, bumping and rebounding with Fool silliness; harnessed by ropes like dray-horses, a platoon of fathers pulled Soap Box Derby contestants; wearing matching scarlet bathing suits and intermittently passed between the shoulders of six brawny men in masks, two platinum blondes held up signs advertising their professional wrestling bouts at the Clear Brook arena the following day; a dozen workers from the Eddy Match Company—the sign for their company made wholly from matchsticks glued onto plywood—tossed out tiny matchboxes from their truck; Rotary Club members clowned, while behind them unsmiling war veterans in uniform walked in formation and stopped every few feet to salute the clapping crowd; and, on the Buckerfield's flatbed, dolled-up ladies sat on hay bales and threw fruit-flavoured candies wrapped in golden cellophane. The Women's Auxiliary and its outpouring of feminine industry—Irish lace, German dirndls, Ukrainian embroidery, Indian saris, and Chinese robes—drew Alberta's applause. "A veritable United Nations," she exclaimed.

The parade closed with another flatbed truck, for Anglo-Am Cedar Products. On it, a clutch of men stood in front of a cedar shake hut; holding chainsaws and shake-splitting axes, they stared down at the thick line of people along the curb with cold eyes and expressionless faces.

Once the Anglo-Am men had passed, the freed spectators milled on 1st Avenue, amused to annex a territory ordinarily reserved for automobiles. Watching the miscellany of townsfolk, Winston was struck by the memory of Dickie asking him about his *fetching get-up* as though he'd recently arrived from a dustbowl Okie settlement with a piece of straw stuck between his teeth. The nerve of that man! What authority did he have? Winston had read enough literature to understand that city sophistication had long been pitted against country simplicity. Indeed, for eons, their faults and strengths had been simplified and exaggerated, so that they became flattened symbols, cartoons no different from those preposterous professional wrestlers, The Strangler and Mr. Marvelous, evil and good; as though any matter could be so cut and dried.

Winston imagined that for certified city dwellers such as Dickie and company, ridiculing country ways might be as habitual a response as taunting was to Alberta upon seeing a jumpy travelling salesman at the door. That attitude must be merited, after all: the country bumpkin was a universal figure of fun. And he felt such disdain from time to time. Likewise, he supposed that Delilah Pierce would venture *cynical*, *superficial*, and *cruel* if she'd spent an hour or two with the gang at the Bamboo Terrace. She wouldn't be wholly in error, either.

Winston squinted his eyes, imagining he could see the essence of the woman walking before him. His vision blurred and he bumped into the man next to him.

"Pardon me," he said, "this is some crowd." The man

nodded. Winston thought the stranger had likely come to the Bend for the derby.

He directed his attention to his mother and Doc Carter, whose youthful feet had moved them a few paces ahead. Winston squinted again for a moment. It was hopeless; there was no single property that defined those two as *belonging* here. And if he looked at himself with objective eyes, he was certain he'd encounter a bubbling stew of properties, each of which might be considered a country or city attribute. That would be the same for each and every man, woman, and child on 1st Avenue.

"Winston, you're dilly-dallying," Alberta said, breaking him from his reverie. "Come join us so that we can find a good view at the bandstand." She clapped her hands together. "Chop chop."

The band onstage was a quartet that featured a plain chestnut-haired woman dressed in a strawberry print calico who could belt out a tune. She sang a pair of mournful ballads about love—won then lost—before turning the stage over to the musicians. They broke out with a polka for the nimble-footed.

Alberta stood between Doc Carter and Winston. She pointed across the still sparsely populated field of dancers— farmers and their wives in their Sunday best were always the first to cut a rug—so that her companions could not help but see her precise target.

"There's Delilah Pierce. Look how she's swaying. I had no idea she was such a romantic."

"Yes, Mother, that's Delilah."

"She'd appreciate your asking her to dance, I'll bet."

"From one of the town's eligible bachelors, no less, a true honour," Doc Carter chimed in with a smirk.

"The bachelor librarian and the widowed Social Studies teacher. Now there's a picture. That'll get tongues wagging, you know." Winston could feel himself being corralled by decorum.

"Let them wag. What's the harm? You two are a tad old for a shotgun wedding, anyway." She smiled at her impertinence.

"Perhaps you're right, Mother. What's one dance, after all?"

Doc Carter joined in with their patter. "And one good turn deserves another, madame. Will you do me the honour?" He bowed slightly, the gesture's sincerity flecked with mockery.

"I will gladly partake when they play the next waltz. That polka is a tad quick for these old pegs, though." She gave her thigh a slap.

"Very well. I'm going to fetch us some punch. Would you like strawberry? Or perhaps strawberry?"

"I'll take strawberry, please."

"Winston?"

"I'm fine, Doc, but thank you for asking."

Doc Carter turned toward the refreshment booth next to the stage and walked along the unmarked line that separated the dancers from the spectators.

"Well, Mother, it's my turn to brave the crowd." Winston nodded at Alberta and started toward Delilah Pierce.

As he approached the house—its glass-flecked stucco dap-
pled by fluttery cottonwood leaf shade—Winston reminded himself to drag the garden hose to the hydrangeas that
stood like wilting regimental guards on each side of the
Manor's front steps. This Indian summer was taking its
toll. He walked to the side gate to check in on Alberta. At
this time of the year, he'd complained to her, she practically lived out of doors. It was no surprise now to find her
hunched over like a seasoned strawberry picker in what she
called her vegetable patch. Winston preferred to think of it
as the acreage.

In past seasons, she'd joked that she had no choice, that
the garden demanded its *Lebensraum* and that she was pow-
erless, the hapless instrument of its infernal design. Now,
with the exception of a rectangular strip of lawn running
alongside the house, vegetables, herbs, and flowers sprouted
everywhere, coaxed into the peculiar shapes and alliances
by Alberta's singular logic—marigolds running in parallel
rows with carrots; zinnias and tomatoes intermixed promis-
cuously, all bordered by purple-leafed sage; towering hol-

lyhocks with cucumbers sprawled at their heels; weedy dill competing with fronds of overgrown asparagus dotted with red berries; beauty pageant contestant dahlias left by themselves to proclaim their poise and beauty.

She had set out three leathery zucchinis, tough parcels of crocodile green that would soon be rendered into something or other and sealed in jars they would be eating from throughout the stretch of winter months. Treading closer, Winston noticed that next to them sat the day's culls: runty beets, fibrous end of season yellow beans, scabby and scarred tomatoes. They could be pickled or stewed, he knew from experience. Alberta was a firm proponent of "waste not, want not" well after the Depression's scarcity years. She might have faith in progress, but she'd seen enough to suspect that a giant step backward was not an unreasonable expectation.

"Well, if there was a God, October would prove it. Hello, Mother. Another glorious day. How's life in the patch?" Winston lowered the register of his voice when he spoke to her from the distance. Alberta's hearing was not what it had been, she reminded him now and again. She'd accepted it as another sign of creeping senility—inevitable, unavoidable, a fact of nature—and couldn't be bothered to go to the ear man Doc Carter had recommended. Why bother?

This young fellow over in Clear Brook could fit her with a space-age hearing aid, Doc Carter let her know whenever they ran into one another, foxy and persistent in the face of her baffling indifference. Unless, of course, her ears were just stopped up with wax: last week he'd offered to *take a look-see* right there on the sidewalk as people filed by them on 1st Avenue. "It's not, er, unheard of," he had said, apologetic about the stillborn pun, before he proceeded with an anecdote, one of scores Alberta suspected he always kept nearby and handy as cod liver oil. She'd told Winston that the doctor's philosophy of medical advice appeared to be "Why not store up examples of mishaps like preserves in a larder?" After he'd spun out the harrowing tale, Alberta had politely refused his offer of an expert examination. Secure at home, she'd related the embarrassing episode to Winston as well as the lesson-filled story the doctor had leveled at her.

Doc Carter was a man fond of stern finger-wagging and precautionary tales about the dear prices thoughtless patients paid for *not taking care of the basics*. The underlying premise was that things are worse than they appear; thus, in his blood-soaked stories, a stubbed toe became an open invitation to gangrene and a scratched mosquito's bite metamorphosed into the royal road to blood poisoning. Carnage around every corner. "An ounce of prevention...," he'd announce with little provocation.

Winston and Alberta had spoken about the Doc's blood-spilling vignettes of fatal carelessness and decided he made them up to order; they were too plentiful and they always seemed perfectly cut to fit the particular circumstance. Could there truly have been such witless men—mesmerized by overheated engines, whirring fans, and shake-dulled axes—and so large a collection of missing fingers, toes, and ears? Still, the whiff of Old Testament reprimand from the mount did make the stories a thrill. Winston saw that Doc

Carter would make a terrific instructor for the Family Life Education unit. Affable, yet impartial and stern.

It was no accident that, years ago, Doc Carter had been put in charge of delivering the personal hygiene lecture to the enlisted men of the district—young and old alike—before their train trip to the recruitment centre in the city. Depending on where the greenhorn soldiers were destined, he would open with, "Men, there's more to France than can-can girls," or else, "Men, there's more to England than trifle." Though he'd also reserved, "Men, there's more to Japan than geisha girls," he'd never had the chance to use it. Polishing his gold-rimmed spectacles with a pressed white hankie, he'd spoken calmly and about practical considerations right after he had shown the short *Educational Program* made by the Government of Canada, its single reel shared, worn down, and splintered by the municipalities of the Valley. He was proud of his contribution to the war effort and, Winston had heard often enough, he found clever ways to pull it into unrelated conversations.

When that fragile celluloid strip didn't fracture and demand one stop-gap repair after another, the federal government's lesson was fourteen minutes of shock tactics that nevertheless incited hoots of merriment and skittish laughter each time Doc Carter clicked on the projector. In it, an elderly scientist with heavy black glasses and a head of wiry grey hair wrote Latin words and their more commonly known synonyms—*Clap, Morning Drop, Dose*—on a portable blackboard and occasionally tugged on his laboratory coat. His lecture faded and was replaced by the view of a camera seemingly set up in the middle of a military doctor's office. It lingered on the legion of moist and gruesome medical conditions enlisted men had dropped their trousers to reveal. The *pièce de résistance* was a series of brief scenes that depicted conniving women—French, unexpectedly, to judge by their unvarying berets and glasses of red wine—loitering in cafés and taverns. Their glistening painted lips, smoldering eyes, and snug wool skirts could evidently siphon key war strategies from unsuspecting men in mere seconds. After the fifth man had shouted out, "I'd like her to try to outfox me," Doc had vowed to write a letter to the Ministry of Defense with his ideas for improving the film. He thought they should leave pale with fear and not flushed from *bonhomie* and guffaws.

Feeling reminiscent years later, he had joked to Winston that if he could not prevent men from tasting forbidden fruit, he could make damn sure they understood the importance of taking precautions. He'd never reported his success rate.

Alberta had relayed the pertinent bits of the doctor's tale to Winston and thrown in some commentary of her own. Apparently, this teenaged boy (the scion—unnamed, thank you very much—of a local lumber baron, no less) had made a half-hearted effort to hang himself in the garage. His mother had discovered him before he completed the deed. After bursting into tears and then giving him a scalding, blurred-vision talking to, she had driven her sullen, shame-faced child directly to Doc Carter's office for treatment of the rope burns. She knew full well that Doc, famed for his fire and brimstone medical enthusiasm, would worm his way into the heart of the problem (not that it would take an Ellery Queen to make sense of those angry scarlet welts) and give the young man a stern finger-shaking-mouth-tsk-tsking-head-shaking lecture about responsibility and the unquestionable value of life.

The doctor had in fact discovered a secret the mother's pleading could not: the entire problem stemmed from two plugs of wax, each one no larger than a click beetle. The boy's personal hygiene could not be called fastidious, it would seem, and his ears had become so blocked with the amber paste that his hearing began to suffer. He thought it was the end of the world. "The very idea," Alberta had interjected. "It's ludicrous." Impetuous and self-important (he was a rebellious and pig-headed sixteen-year-old and the eldest son of local wealth, and he had taken the town aristocrat role to heart), this scamp had decided that death would be preferable to the ignobility of being deaf. "Imagine dying for something so inconsequential, so simple to remedy," the doctor had said pointedly to Alberta, making the parable's message so plain that even a half-wit would understand.

With imploring eyebrows raised high, Winston had agreed that the doctor was well intended and his concern worth at least taking into consideration.

Alberta had replied impatiently, "Yes, you're right, he was, but I'd know it if ear wax was really my problem."

This late afternoon, Alberta wore her broad-rimmed straw hat and the one-of-a-kind calico gardening apron she'd sewn that had as many pockets and flaps as a fisherman's vest. Surrounded by a dense thicket of staked tomato plants, she gave him a harried clerk's Sir-I'll-be-with-you-in-a-moment wave. Winston admitted that his interest in gardening was dilettantish compared with his mother's. It was a happy arrangement. He was content to dabble in his quadrant and produce a handful of perfect striking blooms every season. Besides, he didn't have the spare hours for upkeep; a garden so expansive would be as demanding as raising a child, he imagined. Alberta had told him countless times over the years that the secret of her gardening success was "getting right in there."

She had no advice—not to mention respect—for Sunday toilers who expected instantaneous results from their gardens and who refused to make social sacrifices for maintenance. Usually young wives and busy middle-aged luncheon-and-committee ladies would drop by with a question or two, all the while gazing wistfully at Alberta's plot and wondering aloud about where they might have gone wrong. "You need to get your hands dirty. It's elementary, my dear Watson," she'd throw in with a loopy English accent after telling them they must dedicate an hour of each day to their plots of vegetables or flowers in order to get to know them. In any case, Winston thought no good would result from possessing his mother's degree of enthusiasm. It would have led to a showdown, the *This town ain't big enough for the both of us* confrontation of a John Ford Western.

One time she explained to him, "Gardening's a two-way street, like a marriage, I suppose. You give and then you get."

"Marriage was not exactly your forte, Mother," he teased.

"You're right there, sonny boy," she said, no hint of levity in her reply.

After she had reached her target in the tangle of tomato plants, Alberta turned to face Winston and replied to his salutation.

"Sorry, I saw another one of the little buggers hiding in there," she said as she gazed briefly into the sky. "It is terrific, yes. I was feeling the exact same thing just a couple of minutes ago. You want to breathe in the air till your lungs burst. Though right now all I've got is that sour tang of tomato vine up my nose."

"Funny, I was walking up Grant Street and had this idea of walking without stopping, just walk and walk, taking in the air and admiring the slant of light. It suddenly seemed like there was no practical reason to be indoors and following my routine." Winston squatted for a moment. Then, uncomfortable with his trousers bunched and his shirt pulled taut, he sat on the damp earth. He untied his shoes and removed them along with his mismatched socks. The soil on the pathway was cool but dry and packed hard as pavement.

Alberta spoke as Winston made himself comfortable. "I suppose it's some animal drive. We sense that soon enough we're all about to hibernate, tucked inside our dim little caves during the winter months and waiting until it's safe or warm enough to go outside again." She picked a tomato and tucked it into a pocket. "It's like we want to capitalize on our outdoor time, store up our acorns, I suppose. Maybe our brains can remember the light and recollect it during the February blues. Or greys." She bent over again and darted her hand into the dense Amazonian growth, sly as a weasel.

"Gotcha, you little dickens," she said. "But for a change you're wanting to be the grasshopper more than the ant. Maybe we can take a walk along the Flats on Sunday; I expect the skies will be clear. After church, though, of course." She winked.

He smiled.

"Say, Frank Polovski dropped off an envelope for you today. From the city. I left it in the kitchen."

"From the city? Perhaps it's news from the specialist," Winston said.

"No, it was a Mr. Williamson."

"I can't guess who that could be."

"Well then, you got a letter from someone you haven't met," she said. "Though it's a miracle it ever arrived here."

"I'll be back in a second," he said. He brought his shoes and socks with him to the back door.

Winston returned with an unstamped envelope addressing

*Mr. Winston Wilson*
*River Bend City, British Columbia*

It had a Vancouver return address:

*Mr. Richard Williamson*
*401 - 1585 Georgia Street*
*Vancouver, British Columbia*

"Oh. Dickie. Mother, it's something from that eccentric fellow I told you about months ago. The one I ran into again at the Hudson's Bay on that day we spent in the city." He stood now and spoke from the edge of the path. Alberta had remained still in order to hunt in her tomato plants.

"What's it about?"

The card in the envelope was a party invitation.

A newspaper headline had been snipped in half and scotch-taped to the front of the plain white card:

### Starlet Fails to
### Save Errol Flynn

The newspaper's headline practically shouted its strange accusation. Who would expect a blonde teenaged girl—a Hollywood movie starlet, not a student nurse, nor even a candy striper—to revive a hefty middle-aged man with malaria and a pickled liver who had just suffered a heart attack? Winston thought it was doubtful that a doctor could do so. Flynn's unheroic death at a fancy hotel in the city had made news just weeks before; it had also incited *wages of sin* tongue-clucking in the staff room.

Another clipping had been stuffed inside. Winston unfolded it and examined the grainy newsprint photograph. The **EXCLUSIVE PICTURE** featured Errol Flynn seated—according to the caption—next to "protégé Beverley Aadland, 17." The photograph had been "taken shortly before the film star's death." It was evidently a snapshot, and not a remotely flattering one. He was paunchy, wan, and grizzled, his hair uncombed and face unshaven; it was as though he had not been a swashbuckling, larger-than-life movie actor, but a belligerent professional wrestler who had been on a bender for a few days: tip-toe around him or else pay the price. His wiry protégé might be his shining innocent daughter, blithely enjoying a poolside afternoon at the neighbour's, a barbeque smoking just outside the picture's frame. She wasn't, of course; thanks to tabloids, everyone had read about Errol Flynn's proclivity for starlets and wild Babylonian parties. He was legendary, thought Winston. He reconsidered. Out of respect for Hadrian and Theseus, he decided that *infamous* was better, an accurate evaluation. Being a lecherous lush was hardly a ticket to the heights of Mount Olympus.

Another clipped-out headline—**Flynn 'Old, Sick Before His Time'**—was stapled atop the photograph of the sorry spectacle. Winston smiled at Dickie's handiwork. He thought for a moment that the newspaper's exposure of the actor's ignoble final moments was cruel and gloating. An instant later he recanted, imagining that *live by the sword, die* *by the sword* was perhaps apropos. Errol Flynn was obviously still proud if he allowed for even one photograph of himself with his ample belly spilling over the waistband of his tight-as-sausage skin swimming trunks, full highball glass resting on the ledge of his sea lion's midriff. And besides, Winston thought, all of his fans would remember the countless heroes their hero had played during his prime.

Winston felt sure that if he happened to be wandering around shirtless—perish the thought—he would encourage no one to aim a camera in his direction. And he'd kept his shape far better than the star. Modesty should not be a trait that only women possess, he believed.

Winston walked along one of the packed mud trails of the vegetable patch to hand the clipping to Alberta, still busy ferreting out fat green worms hidden but dangerous in the cluster of tomato plants. With a huff, she exclaimed, "Little beggars, this'll teach you a lesson." She straightened up and dropped her tightly curled captives onto the dirt, tamping the worms back into the earth with the gardening pole. Grendel darted out—tail twisted into a panicked question mark—spooked by the sudden pounding. He paused at the garden's edge and flopped over.

"Okay, that's that—for today at least," Alberta said. She slipped off her gloves and stuffed them into her vest.

"What's this?" she asked as she accepted the envelope from Winston. "Hell, he really went to pot, didn't he? I remember him in *Captain Blood*. So handsome. I knew a couple gals who saw that picture a dozen times over. Joined fan clubs. Odd thing to do when money's so tight. Yes, sir, they'd just swoon whenever he'd pick up a sword. What's this all about, though? Was this Dickie fellow a big fan too?"

"No, Mother, I don't think so." Winston had already looked at the card's remaining content, and was impressed to discovery that calligraphy was one of Dickie's talents. The upper half of the card was filled with two large words—

*Errol Flung!*

The lower half offered an explanation—

*His 'Wicked, Wicked Ways'*
*A Masquerade*
*To Commemorate\* the Sad Passing of a*
*Hallowed Matinee Idol*
*October 31, 1959, Banff House*
*Arrive in Character*

*\* A bottle of his favourite (vodka) will get you past the door*

He handed the card to Alberta.

"'Arrive in character', hey?" she said. "Sounds like your kind of event. You've always been so keen on Halloween." Alberta's sarcasm was shot through with affection.

"I know. A masquerade is bad enough."

"Do you think you'll go? There's very little time. It seems awfully extravagant to head all the way to the city for a party. And such a morbid one. No doubt there'll be one at the school?"

"There is, that's true. It's not the same, though." Winston hoped Alberta would not press him to explain. He felt a child's urge to stamp his feet. "Extravagance is in order sometimes, don't you think? I'm going to think about it, in any case. And I'd be broadening my social circle as one ought, right?"

Alberta patted down stray hairs lifted by the breeze. "I suppose. The big question, if you go, is who will you be? You could show up as that turbaned fellow in *Kim*, maybe, that'd be a cinch to put together. Just sheeting, no stitching to speak of."

"I think turbans are more your style, Mother. Maybe you should come with me—as the agent in *Kim*. Now that I'd like to see."

"Not this time around, my dear. My bones are too weary. Besides, someone has to make sure those hooligans from up the street don't throw eggs—or worse—because nobody's answering the Manor's door. That's one mess I refuse to clean up." Alberta had reached an age when she felt quite comfortable regarding all youngsters as being disrespectful in a way that men in her generation would never have dreamed. She acted scandalized, but Winston had no clue whether she was serious.

She handed Dickie's card back to Winston. "Remember what happened to those Jehovah's Witnesses on 3rd. Bet they really thought the end was coming after that night. Ha! And that was because they had not been at home to deposit candy into grubby little paws." The egging of that house three years back had been front-page news in the

*Record*, citizens—including the mayor himself, who called for a six p.m. curfew—writing searing letters of condemnation, only to be met by others offering rationales or justifications. *Boys will be boys* had been the final albeit unsatisfactory consensus.

"I'll have to think about it. I'm certain that I don't want to wear anything Civil or World War. Nothing seafaring, either." The pulsing excitement he felt across his chest told him the decision had been made. The distant mysteries of Dickie's abode—its cedar red Pomeranians, valuable porcelains, and unknown odours, textures, and decor—stood nowhere close to the hoard Egyptologists had encountered in desert pyramids, but they'd held Winston's interest for months. Now, a room packed with strangers, he thought, that was less relishable. "I wonder if Errol Flynn ever played a farmer?" he wondered. "Now, that would be an ideal costume."

The streets were silent as clouds as Winston passed by houses clutching a brown paper grocery bag tightly under his arm. It contained the costume he and Alberta had cobbled together; he'd wrapped the leggings around his party offering—the transparent bottle of Russian vodka he'd purchased earlier in the week—and wanted to guarantee its safe passage.

Winston saw no raucous children. He spotted a pair of cowboys seated next to their father in a stalled car, but not one half-sized witch, skeleton, scarecrow, or fairy crossed his path. And, he guessed, all the adults were already well on their way to the kind of tomfoolery and future regrets that their drinking and once-a-year guises would encourage. An anxious sensation seeped into his consciousness and settled in his belly like a stone. He hoped spontaneity would not exact some awful price from him. Oughtn't he, an old dog, be rewarded for trying a new trick? Isn't that how it worked?

Hiking along the sidewalk, Winston breathed in the crisp October air, and gratefully drew pleasure from the banks of fog and the occasional bracing assault of rank brine drifting in from the sea. Hearing a sedan bursting with rowdy celebrants, he wondered how hard Dickie, playing impresario, would try for tipsy Flynn verisimilitude, and whether there would be something other than hard liquor for guests to swill. "If it was my party…," he muttered, and then chortled, knowing full well that a party was the very last thing he would ever plan, never mind go so far as hold. Being in the thick of a congregation of fair-weather friends, polite-conversation work colleagues, and townie acquaintances in one cramped room was something Alberta might actually choose; for him, it was too taxing—and for the life of him he could think of no benefits.

If his host strived for realism, it would be too much, Winston sensed, at least if Dickie relied on the sorts of sources his mother had at hand. Alberta, sometime devotee of *Confidential* and its gutter-minded rivals, had been thrilled to present her son with racy bulletins about the rumour, innuendo, and matters of public record that had been dogging Errol Flynn since well before he arrived in Tinseltown. She reported that his early years had been taken up with countless scrapes involving errant wives and their protective, quick-to-see-red husbands, or else precocious young ladies and their outraged parents. When not being caught in the wrong bedroom—or on the criminal side of the age of consent—the man seemed to have been mesmerized by improbable and obviously shady get-rich-quick gold rush schemes in the South Seas; and they had tipped now and again into fraud or theft, involving police and pressmen with cameras in droves.

So the tabloids claimed. Discretion was apparently not part of this adventurer's valour. Later, it was constellations of starlets, entire cases of hard liquor, and frequent men-only fishing trips aboard his yacht, Alberta had relayed, her interest in him dissolving rapidly. She expected her stars to keep their scandals fresh and evolving. Otherwise, their condition was ordinary and sad, too similar to everyday life—like rabbity Mr. Carlton and his chronic problem with drinking before, during, and after work at the post office: pathetic, not exotic, and certainly not titillating.

Winston thought he'd be happy to nurse a bottle of beer and stand a safe distance from the party's teeming middle. That way he could savour the details of his surroundings. Now, no more than a few blocks from the address, he wondered if he should have brought a bottle or two for himself. Not that there'd be any place open this late.

The moment he spotted Banff House he knew it was

too late for all these speculations. "You've made your bed," he told himself. A handful of individual apartments in the building's four storeys were festooned with strands of coloured bulbs and jack-o'-lanterns that stared out from windows with candle-lit faces—leers, smiles, grimaces, orange spike teeth bared. Winston did not need to guess which one of them he was going end up in; he had to raise his eyes just a few degrees. On the top storey, the flat and regular tan brick face of Banff House was fitted with a pair of elaborate Greek balconies, each complete with a combination of dwarf balustrade, pilaster, and pediment. Winston fancied that they could be entrances to a cramped and fussy Doric temple, one which supplicants must reach by air. A movie poster—from the distance he recognized a scene from *The Roots of Heaven*—had been attached to the southernmost balcony. Evidently, Errol Flynn's ponderous African adventure was his destination. A regiment of pith helmets was sure to greet him.

Two women stood at the balustrade, looking toward the city's core, pointing out sights and laughing. Maid Marian and Elizabeth I, Winston presumed, surprised to see them at all. He had not dwelled for long pondering the party's guest list, but he'd imagined that the rooms would be populated by a wall-to-wall corps of Errol Flynns—all friends of the gang. His calculations had a visible flaw.

When Winston pressed **4 0 1** *R.W.* no voice answered, but the whole entrance buzzed like a stove timer. He opened the door and stepped across the threshold. Beside having a floor of tiny white tiles bordered with a black interlocking key pattern and a cedar-framed mural celebrating the epic grandeur of a Rocky Mountain vista—outlandishly, impossibly epic, Winston noticed, because the scale was skewed—the lobby offered him a simple choice: a boxy bronze elevator or a sinuous wooden banister. He supposed the exertion from climbing stairs would help relieve tension, and started toward the narrow staircase.

Winston pulled open the door and stepped into the top storey's hallway, papered with an ivy and trellis pattern; the scant light seeping from the wall sconces completed the greenhouse atmosphere. His stomach had knotted in discomfort and he felt overheated, as though afflicted with a fast coursing fever. Halting his pace, he realized that turning around and leaving was an option. Nobody could tell the difference; Dickie had probably sent the invitation out as an afterthought and would have no way to ascertain whether his casual gesture had actually found its way to River Bend City. And since Alberta was surprised that her son had even chosen to accept Dickie's offer, she would understand his last minute change of heart. He needn't tell her anything, in fact. But he trudged on, ideas like *get some spine* and *old dogs can be taught new tricks* running through his head. Besides, he told himself with an affected nonchalance, what's the worst that can happen?

He stood at the black door. Below the numerals **4 0 1** screwed to its surface, someone had tacked on a copy of the newspaper clipping Dickie had sent with the invitation. Drawing a deep steady breath, Winston knocked.

Almost immediately, a blonde woman in pigtails swung

open the door and stepped inside the frame. Rose petal perfume wafted from her skin. She smiled with lips coloured an intense plum; her loose-fitting man's shirt was knotted high at the waist, brazenly opened at the neck. She was wearing scarlet Capri pants and white ballet slippers. Her left eye was blackened, as though she were a brawler or hitched to a husband who had turned out to be an unfortunate choice. Leaning against the door's frame, she cocked her hip into a mannequin pose and slid her hand up to the topmost corner.

"Hi y'all," she said with a whispery drawl. "I'm Peggy La Rue Satterlee. Truly pleased to meet your acquaintance." She held out her left hand. "And just who are you, sir, and what's there in the bag?" Tendons suddenly relaxed, she dropped her wrist and pointed toward him with a painted index fingernail. Winston was not sure if he should shake her hand, kiss it, or gently clasp it like a minister would with a wife in mourning. He felt his face throb with racing blood even as he remained still.

He said, "Hello. I'm Winston Wilson." The woman's face remained blank, uncomprehending. "I'm trusting that I have not shown up at the wrong address for a costume party." He lifted the brown paper bag to show her that his costume supported his claim. The newspaper clipping is right there on the door, as plain as day, he thought. Sweat was seeping across his forehead; he could sense its unwelcome warmth.

"Tarnation. You don't look like anyone I know." She leaned forward, as though to make a closer inspection.

Winston could now see that she was less young than he had imagined. Impressively made up with foundation and rouged contours, from five feet away and under low wattage she could pass for some American gamin, a charming country girl, sweet if a touch ragged at the edges. At this intimate distance the mirage faded.

She pulled back and swept her eyes along Winston's length from freshly polished shoes to neatly parted hair.

He felt his eyes burrowing insistently. Past the crisp white cotton of her Daisy Mae hillbilly's half-unbuttoned shirt, they found the murky black filigree straps and scalloped lace cups of her brassiere.

"They're real you know, honey," Peggy La Rue Satterlee said.

He looked into her eyes. Sweat trickled along his temples.

She grasped and then fondled the pearls strung around her neck. "Yes, sir, 100% cultured. You can touch them if you want. That's the only way to know for sure, ya touch them. If they're costume: smooth as silk because they're plastic, Oriental imitations. But if they come from a shell, they're ever so slightly grainy."

"Thanks, I'll take your word for it." Winston was mortified that she'd noticed him staring.

"I declare, I remember it like it was yesterday." She clenched them in her hand and closed her eyes, apparently deep in fond memory. "Errol fawned all over me, you see, and gave them to me on his yacht when we were taking a weekend jaunt to Mexico. 'A memento,' he told me." Her eyes opened and adjusted themselves into a peeved squint. "Then, no more than ten minutes later, he bashed me one, the pie-eyed jackass. I tell ya, he coulda saved himself a whole boatload of grief if he'd been nicer to me. He gets me real steamed. To this day. I tell ya! I got him, though, didn't I? I slapped his face so hard his ears rang like church bells. And that's not all." She had softly rested a hand on her bruise as she described her run-in.

Winston stood in the hall and felt his embarrassment spreading as her volume steadily rose. Peering down the hall, he fully expecting to see angry heads poking out from neighbouring doors. No one was bothered by this apparition's voice, apparently. He tried to peek inside the room, but the lighting was low compared to the hallway.

"And then like some kinda *souteneur*, he tries to pass me off to a couple of his buddies, really browned me off. I may be friendly, but I'm not that sorta gal. All my sweet Southern hospitality gets misunderstood by black-hearted Yankee bastards." She pressed a finger into Winston's coat. "You ain't a Yankee, I suppose?" she asked.

Winston's ears were blazing and his smile felt like a suit that he'd outgrown. He looked past her shoulder again, now imagining that he was being rude.

"Oh my, now where are my manners? That man just gets me in such a state. A real bane. Gets stuck in my craw like a cat's hair. C'mon in, honey, I'll show ya around." Hips still cocked she beckoned him into the party. As Winston passed she rested her hand briefly on his lower back and patted it.

Once Winston was inside, the hostess closed the door and heaved herself against the coats hanging from hooks on the back. She assumed another suggestive pose. Winston stifled a smile, imagining that she aspired to be Marilyn Monroe and had rehearsed all those trademark wiggles and routines for untold hours in front of a closet door mirror. Glancing around, he noticed that cigarette smoke floated in cirrus cloud layers throughout the living room. Miss Satterlee grasped his lapels.

"They're rice, you see." The voice had changed. In that fraction of a minute Winston saw that he was face to face with Dickie. It was so obvious, he realized. So why hadn't he noticed it before? It must be some trick of nerves or light. He grinned. "I'll be damned. That's some costume!" Unlike Delilah, who had dressed as Florence Nightingale for the high school's afternoon Halloween social, Dickie's transformation had forged a newly born personality. He could pass convincingly as another person, and as the opposite sex. Winston was startled but entranced by the effect.

Dickie had untied the shirt to reveal that no breasts were covered by those silky lace cups. "One scoop per, then tucked into my brassiere," he said. Up close, Winston could see faint grains pressing against the surface of the taped waxed paper breast. They sat atop Dickie's smooth skin, from which not a single hair sprouted, Winston was surprised to discover.

"That's fascinating. You had me utterly convinced. For a moment. I'd like to look again in better light," he said. His intense feverishness subsided. From behind Dickie, he could hear boisterous voices and orchestral surges alongside Dinah Washington's crying the blues.

"'Better light'? Oh no, my dear. For my purposes, this sort of twilight is best," Dickie explained. "Too much destroys the illusion, as any woman knows."

"And the bruise is illusion too?"

"Midnight Rendezvous and Parisian Prune, that's all." Dickie's modesty was unexpected.

"Calligraphy and secret disguises, Dickie. Is there no limit to your talents?" Winston opened the bag and handed his host the bottle of Russian liquor. "Here, this is to get me through the door."

"Goodness, from all the way behind the Iron Curtain. Is it safe to drink?"

"I'm sure it is. I hope it will serve your needs." He ran his eyes around the room. "Incidentally, are your twin dogs nearby?"

"I can introduce you to them later if you'd like. Right now they're secure with Mrs. Gillis downstairs. Just for the record, farmer, I'm Peggy La Rue Satterlee—cheap actress, statutory rape victim extraordinaire, courtroom star witness—for the night. I made Flynn's life a misery in the '30s. And, buster, why the hell are you still Winston?" Dickie was adjusting the straps of his brassiere as he spoke.

"I couldn't very well come over dressed like a fool." He felt silly and unadventurous as he spoke such words in reply to a fellow dressed as a buxom if bruised Southern starlet.

"It's Halloween, honey. Nobody would notice a thing."

"If you give me five minutes to change, I'll be a new man."

"Very well, just this one time I'll give you a break."
Dickie bent over in an acrobatic flourish, one hand running
down the back of Winston's legs, and untied his shoes. He
said, "Here, this'll give you a head start," then righted himself and smiled.

A changed voice drawled, "I declare, my dear, we ought
to get y'all to the powder room." He sashayed away, all hips
and winks. "Walk this way," Peggy La Rue Satterlee said
with a smirk, swaying enormously en route to the bathroom. Like a desert mirage, Winston thought. He could
see both illusion and truth simultaneously, the Miss Satterlee persona—sashaying, purring, winking—outermost, and
Dickie's silhouette and wicked sense of humour barely beneath. These few minutes had him already feeling distressed.
Winston kept his eyes trained on his sanctuary destination,
blind for the moment to all other movement in the room.
Miss Satterlee warbled *worship the trousers that cling to him*
alongside Dinah Washington.

"Here you go," said Dickie, opening the door. "And
while I'm here, let me take care of your coat."

Winston closed the door with relief. He heard muffled pulses of party noise, but still felt damp and uncomfortable. His brain had turned haywire. At the mirror over
the sink he was relieved to find his everyday face and no
tell-tale outward sign—febrile flush, scarlet ears, Mr. Hyde
eyes. He bent to the sink—both mirror and basin were too
low, as though the bathroom had been built for children or
with grief-shrunken East European widows in mind—and
splashed his face with cold water.

Face dripping, he reached for a hand towel on the door. The bathroom was clean and uncluttered, he noticed. Borderless white tile floor, dull rose bathtub and toilet, lace curtains over a frosted glass window, a small black radiator with its filigree design highlighted in gold. He kicked off his shoes. He took a step to closely examine the two gaudy portraits of seated poodles in profile, both grey and white: paint-by-number. Their frames were painted gold. A few bottles of aftershave rested on a doily atop the toilet tank along with dried creatures of the deep—two sand dollars, a starfish, a sea urchin. He would gladly wager that the intense lung pink on the walls had been Dickie's selection.

Winston could tell that he was procrastinating, and began unbuttoning his shirt. He removed and folded his trousers, and placed them on the lid of the toilet seat. He lodged his cufflinks deep in a trouser pocket and set his shirt atop. The strangeness of the circumstance gave him pause. Giddily, he considered his predicament. Here he was, standing practically naked in the bathroom of a mere acquaintance and about to put on a costume and talk with other complete strangers dressed as characters played by a dead movie star to whom he'd never paid close attention. The whole imposing scene made a trip to the Belle-Vu seem like child's play.

It was the kind of predicament Lucille Ball would stumble into, he decided. The difference was, his adventure would not neatly wrap itself up by the end of a half-hour episode. It might not be side-splittingly funny, either. Though he had attended exactly three costume parties over the years in the Bend, he'd done nothing like this before; it was nerve-racking, but he trembled with excitement too.

Winston returned to the mirror and ran his index finger along its scalloped top. There was no dust. So close that he could not see his face, his view ran from the band of his underpants to the shoulder straps of his undershirt. As always, he was taken aback and dismayed by the tenacious hairs—tendrils like black moss—that leapt from beneath the edges of the undershirt's smothering field of white. He posed, arms sharply angled in the Charles Atlas style, and noticed the pungency of his armpits. Nerves.

Other librarians he had met were soft stoop-shouldered men heading toward jelly or else stick-like and abstemious, but Winston recognized that he was trim and firm, robust even. In the mirror, he could not help tracing the halo of fur on his arms, shoulders, and neck. Alberta had it right when she had talked about animals and hibernation; his coarse dense pelt would certainly bring to mind the word "ursine." Ursa Major, he thought, indulging in a nonsense thought of himself arranged as a heavenly constellation. That hair had the good sense to quit, thankfully. His nose remained properly fallow and pink and his ears showed no sign of pig's bristle. And the hair had its benefits: unlike his colleagues—struck hard and frequently by chills, colds, coughs, and complaints between November and March—he was never bothered by low mercury in winter and only rarely ambushed by the maleficent germs that lurked like kamikaze pilots in the high school's corridors.

"Dilly-dallying," he reminded himself, using one of

Alberta's longstanding favourite words of approbation. He opened the bag that held his costume. For shoes, Alberta had sewn him moccasins from brown felt. He had bought thick leather bootlaces, and wound them in for an authentic touch. At least narrow strings of animal hide seemed apt. It might be closer to Robin Hood than Edward, they had conceded, but those two Englishmen were not that distant, historically speaking. Besides, shoes? What did they wear then, who could say? The illustrations from history books revealed a Jesus-haired bearded man with a perfectly aquiline nose who wore a bandeau and fortified his vulnerable body with a heavy cape or else a jupon emblazoned with elongated lions and fleurs-de-lis. Masons shaping his likeness at Canterbury Cathedral hadn't cared much about footwear; they were trifling details, Alberta had decided. It was the regal countenance staring bravely into the afterlife that mattered. For posterity, and all that.

Winston looked down at the leggings, then at his underpants—a recent invention, surely. A Victorian development, most probably: sensible and decorous. He could not recall any book he'd read in which underwear was mentioned. It was unmentionable. He snorted. Stop by stop, Hadrian's tours of the far reaches of Rome's empire had been duly recorded, but knowledge of his intimate apparel was forever lost. Invisible. Beneath all that leather and chain-mail and wool padded with horse hair, what was there? If his own underwear proved to be an anachronism, he would live with it. He'd feel too exposed without any. He was no Errol Flynn, after all, prepared to shuck his clothes and leap stark naked into water without a moment's hesitation, alone or amidst a crowd of onlookers. That might be the reason for all the drink, Winston thought. Magnificent Captain Blood's secret weapon: high jinks and courage available by the bottle.

Drawing the rest of his clothing from the bag, Winston had small hopes that he could pull off costume and character. He'd pored over a few books in the library to get a deeper understanding of Edward the Black Prince, and had come to learn only that historians made him fit into the standard heroic mould, less an actual breathing person than a type or ideal. Winston had also grown to think of Edward as sullen and enigmatic since all the images he'd encountered were dour funerary effigies, carved in stone or cast in bronze or plaster and fastened to joyless church walls and family tombs.

He'd guessed a historian studying the fourteenth century was not faced with a surplus of evidence to sift through, and concluded that it was no surprise that Edward's personality was muted and so indistinct. It wasn't as though the Black Prince had left a diary so that future generations could read about his innermost hopes and desires. He was no gushy, self-dramatizing schoolgirl. Nor an ink-happy Augustine roiled by guilt. Edward's was an era of grave talk and decisive action, not poesy and romantic navel-gazing. A question like, "How do I feel today?" or "What is the meaning of existence, I wonder?" had probably never been forged in his stalwart's head. Centuries after the fact, no one could say what he *felt*. What time was there for feeling when there was territory to safeguard or seize? Small wonder the history books painted such a hazy picture.

Alberta had sewn a padded tunic for Winston after he'd decided a cape was too showy. It was an approximation based on a photograph he had located in a Bend school district textbook, *The Ancient and Medieval World*. The jupon, as they'd learned to call the garment, had originally been worn as protection from the rain that caused armour to blossom with rust. It had also prevented the wearer from sizzling like a barbecued steak during summertime skirmishes.

Winston pulled the jupon over his head, and struggled with its tight awkward shape. Why had buttons taken so long to be invented, he wondered? Judging the final result, Alberta had recommended a red satin diagonal sash because the costume was drab, the wormy brown of mud flats. It gave him a menial appearance. With a smirk she'd said, "Needs a splash of royal pomp. You look like you scrub castle chamber pots." He pulled at the sash until the seam aligned with his hip.

Standing at the mirror, he puffed up his chest in mock-heroic style. He mussed up his hair. Edward might have been gaunt, club-footed or pigeon-chested, Winston imagined. Books had offered little guidance; Edward was a heroic warrior who may or may not have earned his name by girding himself with black armour. *C'est tout*, as Alberta said. Fond of pig's liver, a wandering night owl, possessing a pronounced lower lip or missing teeth: no researcher would ever uncover those significant details. What else was there to interpret? He lived with lineages, foes and friends, strategies, alliances, and battles, some won, some lost.

Winston supposed he would be highly disciplined and even prone to violent outbursts and drunken venting. If he even possessed one, his sense of humour would be crude, all sleight of hand and jester pratfalls; otherwise, he would be rigid, uncreative, and demanding, grabbing what he wanted and chucking away anything or anybody in his way. Charismatic, probably. Winston had met a few locals who had become officers during the war, and to a man they were marked by such characteristics, though not as pronounced as they would have been over half a millennium ago. Civilization had advanced, at least on the surface. Then as now, success in the military would come easier to some personalities than others, Winston thought.

Besides, he wasn't meant to be Edward, but rather the Black Prince as acted in front of a camera by Errol Flynn pronouncing words he'd half-learned—the star's inability to prepare for scenes and remember lines was another notorious tidbit Alberta had fed him—from a screenplay written by some man who might have consulted the same books Winston had skimmed through. And all of it on a wood and plaster of Paris stage in sunny California. The liberties taken were no doubt as enormous as the gap between flesh and blood actuality and the mute carved figure on a tomb in England.

If nothing else, Dickie's Peggy La Rue Satterlee had made it clear that rifle-range accuracy was not the true goal. Inspired performance was. Winston frowned, thinking he might get by with an occasional *thee* and *thou* sprinkled into his conversation. It's not as though anyone would think to criticize him; it was irreverent and fun, he thought. That pixie notion of silliness was what he'd already come to admire about this group. He decided that a few references to the times—the Black Death, the Hundred Years Wars, the bastard French king—would keep partygoers occupied. Plague would be better than war for a few stories—nobody would care a fig about a century of complicated skirmishes and shifting alliances that occurred thousands of miles away over 600 years ago. But disaster and strife always keep people riveted, regardless of the epoch; older folks still spoke in reverent tones of the devastating Spanish influenza of the Great War. He would describe the lingering deaths of helpless servants and courtiers. Religious mania and bizarre rites of mortification. Filthy straw beds hopping with fleas. He'd throw in roaming packs of vermin too. Corpses with *rigor mortis*. There were definite possibilities.

A rapid-fire knock on the bathroom door interrupted his forecasting. "Almost finished in there, Gorgeous George?" a man's voice asked.

"Oh, I'm sorry," he said, his mouth close to the door. "I'll be just a minute."

He used a kohl pencil Alberta had purchased for him to draw a moustache, and then speedily sketched in a hairy point on his chin, smoothing away the clean edge of the lines with his fingers. He could have grown a beard in a week, but it made him feel unkempt and ragged. Kohl would wash off in a second. With hurried and rough strokes, he parted his hair in the middle. Even in statuary, Edward's hair was never neatly combed. Alberta's leather and foil bandeau completed the transformation.

Standing back to grasp the full effect in the mirror, he pronounced judgment: "Idiotic." He reminded himself of one of the mole-like serfs of *The Time Machine*. "King of the Morlocks."

Winston picked up his street clothes and shoved them in the grocery bag. Looking around for a storage place, he chose the bathtub. They would be secure there.

Swinging open the door, he stared into the hallway. Dressed in a sharply pressed khaki army uniform, the man who had knocked was leaning against the wall. Winston smiled at him and apologized: "Sorry to keep you waiting."

"Don't fret it, squire," the man said as he pressed close to Winston en route to the bathroom.

Winston walked down the short hallway into the living room. As he expected, the room was crowded, filled with conversations, moving bodies, a blue haze of cigarette smoke, and the world-weary voice of Dinah Washington, who while now upbeat was complaining about her run of *bad luck and lousy people*. The woman had such a hard life, if her songs were to be believed.

He saw that two tables had been butted together in a corner. One was cluttered with glasses, bottles, and a miscellany of juice, lemons and limes, an ice bucket, sugar. The other one held oranges, and nothing else. What must have been a box of them had been carefully stacked into a stupendous pyramid. He imagined them as a cairn that announced vital news in a foreign tongue. Winston headed toward the arrangement, curious. It had not tumbled apart and he wanted to find out why.

Someone grasped him by the arm, and Winston turned to see a smiling Johnny, who had also outfitted himself as a one of the many historical Flynns.

"Welcome, dear traveller," Johnny said as he clasped Winston's right hand heartily with both of his heavily ring-laden hands. He looked around the room for a moment and continued: "I hope Dame Slatternly wasn't being a bother at the door. I can have her dispatched post-haste if you desire it, honourable sir. A pox on her scurvy hide." Johnny was dressed in tights and a cape. He wore a woolly beard that seemed to be glued on to his face, which Winston thought was well complemented by his eye patch. Grasping him like they were old buddies, he walked Winston toward the table. Winston realized Johnny was already thoroughly drunk. "You see, that jade hasn't been quite right in the ol' head"— he tapped two fingers against his temple—"since the statutory rape trial way back during the War. Too much fame and attention for her tiny doxy's brain, methinks. As the Bard would have it, *she's is a subtle whore / A closet, lock and key, of villainous secrets.* Ya gotta watch her closely or she'll swallow ya whole."

Winston guessed that Johnny was a swashbuckling pirate. "Captain Blood, I presume?" he asked.

"Sir, you insult me. I am honorable, no bloodthirsty hoodlum. It is I, Robert, Earl of Essex. Yonder is my fair Queen, Elizabeth Tudor." He gestured behind his shoulder vaguely. Winston saw no monarch, fair or dark.

"Let's get you something to drink. Catch up with the rest of us. We came over early to help her set up, and, well, had a few to get us in the mood."

"I was hoping that there might be something with less kick. A bottle of beer perhaps?"

"Oh, no, nothing doing, sire. I'll pour you a mean vodka Collins. Got the recipe from Judy Canova herself. It's fruity and sweet. You won't taste any of the hard stuff in it. Smooth as silk. You'll be fine."

"Thank you, kind sir." At the table, Johnny poured and stirred. Winston gestured toward the display of oranges and asked, "What's this all about?"

"You have to ask Slatternly for the actual details, but on the set of I think *The Roots of Heaven* our man Flynn was trying to dry out … so drunk he could barely stand. Memorizing lines wasn't going too well. So the studio ordered everyone to help out. Prevent him from drinking, more like it. Dumped out his cache of bottles. Watched him between takes. And so on."

Watching Johnny squeeze half a lemon into the shaker, Winston felt his tongue contract. "Anyway, no fool, Flynn had a friend who delivered orchard fresh oranges 'for health,' and they'd all been injected with shots of vodka. Used a hypodermic needle so that no one would suspect a thing. Kept him suitably pie-eyed while the studio imagined he was on the road to clean and sober living. So they're atomic oranges, I guess."

"Here, this nectar will cure what ails you." Johnny handed the tall glass to Winston. *Love bloomed like a flower, and then the petals fell*, sang Miss Washington.

They clinked glasses. "Salut," Johnny said.

"To your health," Winston said, and took a trial sip. The cocktail was tangy yet sweet, just as Johnny had promised, and yet had no kick.

The Earl offered to take the Black Prince on a tour of the kingdom, to study the lay of the land and meet the little people.

Winston in tow, he started toward the balcony. "We'll take a gander at the highlights as well as the lowlights," he said.

Parked in a corner near the balcony, a hairy man wore a belted bathing suit and nothing else. He had apparently brought his own nylon strap lawn chair from which to view the room. Straining its aluminum frame, cocktail resting on his abdomen, he was none other than a tubby Hogarth grotesque or a figure of horror in a wax museum. But animated, an automaton. Winston did not have to guess; he'd just seen the photo on the door. The man's pale eraser nipples leapt out from an inky mat of hair. Winston's eyes were captivated and appalled by the man's companion, who, he knew, might instigate a stampede in the light of day. Deplorable. Here, the infamous protégé was dressed in a short indigo blue kimono kept loosely tied to reveal a bikini, navy blue with yellow polka dots; a fine line of downy hair ran along the soft thin torso. The bikini top was not stuffed and the bottom bulged. The combination was obscene, Winston thought, indecent. As brazen and unnatural as Nero, the fat man rested his hand on his date's hairy and sinewy thigh. Swallowing a titter, Winston chided himself for his lack of sophistication: clearly, no one else saw the scene as untoward.

"Miss Aadland here finds our bustling city by the sea something of a bore," Johnny said to Winston.

"Well, it's no Beverly Hills, I suppose," Winston nodded, sipping eagerly from his cocktail. He was examining the bright yellow strands of wool she wore as hair, and the garish makeup: its over-emphatic colours—pink pearl lips, a rouge orb on each cheek, a dark flock of summertime freckles—were a cartoon of a teenaged girl.

The couple had been speaking to a man with a camera hanging from his neck. He'd turned to Essex and the Black Prince as they came close and blinded them for an instant with the bulb's white flash. "Greetings, gentlemen, Bill McBride, Ace Detective Agency," he'd said, holding out his hand. "The alarmed parents of a certain young lady have hired me to keep an eye out...."

"You know, honey, sometimes you gotta do what you gotta do."

Bette Davis, in a hoop skirt, pouting and spoiled as she had played it in *Jezebel*, was explaining why she'd bothered to make an appearance. A moment before, Winston, feeling looser now that he was nearly finished his second Judy Canova Collins, had mentioned that Errol Flynn did not actually star with her in that movie. He had thought to say she didn't look like Miss Bette, either, but changed his mind. It was rude; and he was certainly no double for Errol Flynn. Still, her makeup was pallid and thick. Pie dough. No hint of Dickie's talent in evidence. Winston had first tried to place her as a nun or a Puritan—all drawn unsmiling features and severely restrained hair—but could recall none from the Flynn repertoire.

Bette held a cigarette between her scarlet-tipped fingers and leaned heavily against the kitchen counter. She radiated gardenia. Turning to her girlfriend Peggy La Rue Satterlee, she exclaimed, "Sister, what sad times we live in. Don't anyone know that a gentleman ought to offer to light a lady's cigarette?"

"Well, you're looking as lovely and sprightly as ever, Bette, but you ain't no lady," Essex said. He held out a lighter and expertly flipped it open.

"Ignore him, Bette. As you well know, he's no gentleman. I wouldn't spend one minute alone with him if I were you. Buyer beware, I say." Miss Satterlee drank from her glass as though it held a nerve-calming tonic.

"Slatternly...." Johnny acknowledged her with audible growl in his voice.

Miss Satterlee thrust out a hand as though she were trying to stop traffic. "Don't you come too close to me, Mr. Leslie Thomas Flynn, or I'll give you something to be sorry for. Again." Winston smiled, astounded to be in the midst of such an unlikely quarrel. "'Sides, I've made a few good friends with fat wallets down at a magazine you're quite familiar with. They're always interested in hearing what fresh news I can dig up for them."

Satterlee grabbed Winston by the arm. "That man, he gets my dander way up. You watch your back."

"We should get a move on, sport," Johnny said, close to Winston's ear.

Directing Winston toward the table of bottles, he added in a loud voice, "Ya gotta wonder if that dame is knitting with both needles."

🦆

"They dropped dead, like flies upon the autumn's first frost. It was a divine message, but we could not fathom the true nature of our mortal sin." While Essex tended to fortifying their drinks, the Black Prince was explaining the rigors of daily life under the pall of the Black Death to a man who had been introduced as "the notorious studio hack, Mr. Michael Curtiz."

During the few moments that he actually spoke, the man spat out words with a German accent. He wore a shimmering red ascot and used a monocle with expert flair. His hair was combed straight back and glistened with grooming oil. Winston continued, spurred on by the director's intent nods: "Elders of our holy church implored us to fast and pray. They dictated that mortification would be our salvation. But still the suckling babes and ancient relics, monstrous sinners and living saints alike, fell into fevers and died twisted in agony." He clutched the man's shoulder.

"We burned them all, denying their souls proper burial in hallowed ground." He was tickled with the picture of devastation he was painting—like something from a Bosch canvas—even though he was no longer sure about the details he kept throwing on.

Curtiz removed the monocle and gripped it in his hand. He exclaimed, "*Éclaircissement*, as za French vould zay! I haf read of zis *Seuche*, but haf never imagined vot a visual spektac-le it vould be. Vot a picture it vould make! Epic! Tragic! Ja, I vill haf to talk mit Herr Varner about dis."

"Gentlemen. I come bearing gifts." Essex was carrying a small metal tray loaded up with their particular mixes of vodka. "Cheers," he exclaimed as the Black Prince and Herr Curtiz reached for their glasses.

"Bevare of creeps bearing gifts, no?" the director said to Winston with a wink.

"Hell of a good party, Essex. Very good. Nice." Ed was dressed in khaki trousers and a rumpled white linen shirt. His hair was parted differently. Winston could see that he'd shed some weight.

"Pleased to meet you. Jake Barnes." He shook Winston's hand. "Edward of Woodstock, eldest of the children of Edward III and Phillipa of Hainault. Keeper of the realm. Sworn enemy of Philip of Valois and all his kin." Winston knew he was drunk and going on, but could see it was funny. He knelt for a moment in mock deference.

"This here's my girl, Georgette. Georgette Hobin. She's French. She's a dancer, damn splendid one. A man would be a fool not to marry her. It's rotten that she's already married."

"Milady," Winston bowed his head.

"Cheers," Georgette said, and tapped her glass to Winston's.

The balcony had become the location for a gathering of historical importance no oracle would have foreseen. Winston was watching General Custer and his wife as they listened to an animated Elizabeth Tudor—the gesticulations of her hands reminded him of an Italian merchant, not an English monarch—and her consort, another Essex. The tableau would prove a challenge for Alberta to capture in her next pillow cover, he thought with a start. He'd have to suggest it, even though she'd surprised him by not being terribly enthusiastic about the antics of the gang that he had relayed so far.

"…and, let me tell you, we had to put a few of the royal jewels in hock after that," Elizabeth was explaining to Custer as Winston approached the balcony. The group erupted with laughter. Staring to the east, he saw the Shell Oil clock and its otherworldly neon glow. The General asked his lady if she would care to dance, and the pair passed by.

He smiled at Elizabeth, but she said nothing and looked

at her suitor. Essex nodded curtly and led the regal consort inside by her raised hand.

Winston turned and watched Johnny nod and say, "Ladies," as he wound his way toward the balcony. Standing next to him, Johnny offered an explanation: "Bull dykes. They tend to keep to themselves. We think they don't really like us men at all. Who can blame them?" Johnny sighed, leaning heavily on the ledge.

Winston watched the women, now amidst the clutch of dancing couples in the living room. They may as well be Martians for all the insight he has about them, he thought. Below the calm—that thinnest of surfaces—stood another person. The Rosenbergs. Lesbians. The murderous lover, Leo Mantha, his mother's former cause. He wondered what he'd learn if he could delve into the mind of Dickie or the skinny fellow wearing the bikini. Even Delilah Pierce and himself. Layer after layer of the same translucency like an onion? Or, as in a jawbreaker, one colour melting away to reveal another?

"What a night, hey," Johnny said. He bumped his hip into Winston's and remained close.

Johnny surveyed the rooftops and contours of distant buildings wrapped by tendrils of fog. Winston remembered Alberta's vision of the prehistoric Valley and had no difficulty seeing murky reptilian heads cutting swaths through the fog. He smiled woozily and leaned against the balcony door. The muscles in his legs felt too feeble to bear his weight.

"My good fellow, you're pie-eyed. And I've barely had a chance to ply you with Judy Canova Collins." He placed a hand on Winston's shoulder. Winston resisted the urge to slide toward the floor.

"Excuse me for a moment, good sir." Winston's belly warned him that if he didn't keep moving he was sure to retch. He was mortified at the thought of it. An inebriated vomiting in plain sight was not a way he had ever imagined humiliating himself. Planted in a corner like a wallflower was his usual role. Whenever Winston turned down her occasional offers of a nightcap, Alberta told him he would have made a good Puritan. And here he was, drunk as a schoolboy. He breathed deeply, measuring the intake to steady his stance.

Errol and Beverly were dancing inside, slowly circling in the living room and interlaced with other lively reincarnations of the recently deceased movie star. Standing at the edge of the crowd, Winston thought that with his bulk and all the hair on his back, the man actually looked like a dancing bear; his bathing trunks were incongruous, like the tiny peaked hat on an organ grinder's monkey. For the scrawny and pale girlish dance partner he could still find no words and resisted an insistent urge to guffaw. Miss Washington tightly held her monopoly on the bittersweet blues, now telling her disappointing lover *you don't know what love is.*

Folds of smoke hung in the air as though fog had crept in from the night. Through the haze, Winston watched the hands of Peggy La Rue Satterlee squeezing an orange at the cocktails table. The revelry—warm perfumed bodies, blustery conversations, and shrieks of laughter—felt overwhelmingly close. Winston was propelled by the sudden belief that he required solitude to restore his calm. If he could locate his coat, he'd slip out like the proverbial thief in the night. It would take just a moment to change his clothes.

He waited in the shadowy hall outside of the bathroom after rattling the doorknob on the closed door. The jack-o'-lantern sitting on the floor gave off a meager light; he did not remember it and wondered if earlier he had been too nervous to pay attention. Feeling slack, he slumped against the wall for support.

Georgette opened the door opposite. Winston gazed past her to see Frankie sitting in profile at the end of the bed, his trousers bunched at his ankles. His shirt was open and Winston's eyes traced the line of hair from his chest downward. Frankie nodded at Winston and a smile spread across his face, evaporating as quickly. He ran his left hand along his taut belly before letting it settle between his legs. Georgette closed the door and hurried toward the party. The door remained shut.

Winston rubbed his eyes with the palm of his hand. Over the music, he heard the bathroom door scrape along the tile floor.

"Have you seen my girl, you know, Georgette?" Ed asked.

"Just walked toward the kitchen, I think." Winston could not open his eyes when he answered.

"Are you feeling alright?"

"I'm fine. Dizzy. Need a minute or two for myself, that's all."

"Just holler if you need anything, my friend."

"Thank you, Ed, I will."

Inside the bathroom—the door shut and locked—he walked to the sink. He was relieved that the mirror reflected nothing unseemly; the bandeau was intact and his drawn-on beard had not streaked. His lips were stained bright from drink.

At the toilet, he struggled with the costume, lifting and holding up the jupon while trying to roll down the leggings and underpants. Leaning with one palm flat against the wall behind the toilet tank and legs spread to keep the leggings secure, he watched the colourless stream jet into the toilet bowl. He chortled at the ridiculous picture he'd make. In real life, Falstaff would be unsightly and pathetic, a boorish guest who'd overstayed his welcome.

Bowel and bladder movements on the battlefield, Winston thought. Now there was another example of the kind of mystery left unsolved by history books. Wishing not to make a mess, he held his member—the *membrum virile* as he had learned to call it in his high school days—and aimed for dead centre. The technique was noisy; it was his habit to strive for silence by directing the stream to the side of the bowl. He could change his ways, though, if it would be a benefit. Splashing over the floor would be almost as bad as vomiting. His manhood felt warm in his hand—flushed, expansive. Another attribute of firewater, he concluded. It was no wonder the stuff caused such havoc when settlers gave it to Indians.

Winston imagined that a few minutes alone would help him regain his composure. He knocked on the bedroom door. No one answered. Curious to know if Frankie had fallen asleep, he turned the doorknob, stepped inside, and quietly closed the door. The heavy curtains were drawn in Dickie's bedroom. Frankie was gone. Winston made his way to the bed, vividly recalling Frankie's posture on the bed and Georgette avoiding his stare as she passed him in the hall. Winston told himself that he'd stretch out on the bed for a moment. He slid off his moccasins and lay down, resting his face near to where he'd watched Frankie.

"C'mon, Sleeping Beauty, you ought to make your presence known to your minions."

"Not too much of a drinker, we see. You need an iron stomach for it, I suppose."

"What's the time?"

"It's late. Everyone's gone home."

"Some fresh air would do us all well. We'll take a walk, see what's going on out there."

"A walk to the Enchanted Forest."

"What's that?"

"C'mon, get your regular clothes on. A brisk trip out of doors will sober you up."

The fog had lifted and the night was starry and clear. He could smell the lingering scent of exploded firecrackers, but Winston heard no vestiges of revelry. It felt like the winter stillness of November had completely settled in with the frost.

"We think you'll love it there, Farmer," Dickie chirped.

"Why is that?" He thought that what he'd love was sleeping off his headache under warm blankets at home.

"Just an inkling, really."

They crossed the street that evidently marked the border between city and park—no other apartment blocks with brightly lit lobbies stood before them—and walked toward a pond over which hung the residue of fog. The men remained silent. Even Dickie kept to himself. Winston guessed that only he among them had no notion of their destination. That put him at a disadvantage.

"It's rather difficult to see," he said as they strode ahead unerringly.

Dickie turned and explained in a loud whisper: "You'll get your sea legs in no time."

In the gloom, Winston was barely able to distinguish the blank darkness of the forest and brush from the star-specked night sky. They walked over an elfin stone bridge; as they approached a road that severed grassy flatland from tenebrous wall of trees, Johnny and Ed huddled to light cigarettes.

Dickie caught up and gestured for Winston to join them. He placed an index finger to his lips. Winston could not fathom where he was heading with these men and wanted to giggle at the ridiculousness of this rendezvous-at-midnight situation. Like Dickie's purple bruise makeup, the silence and cloak and dagger skulking tilted into melodrama. It was trite, but he was hooked by it; the unknowingness had its narcotic effects. Besides, he'd heard, there was nothing like a trip away to make a man appreciate the comforts and routines of home—the idea being that grass would always be greener until it is visited up close.

Dickie clasped Winston by the neck and whispered in his ear: "Here we are." Winston watched the men, now in single file, slip into a passage between two stands of trees. He could not have seen that sliver of an opening himself; these night dwellers apparently had the eyes of cats. He followed closely behind Dickie, exhaling vapour into the frigid air.

They stopped at a place where the trail widened into a grotto. "Stay right here. We're going to wander for a few minutes. But we'll fetch you, so don't fret."

"You want to leave me here? What on earth for?" he whispered. This new part of their plan gave him instant cause for worry.

Dickie once again placed index finger to lip.

Winston could not help but think of the pranks and worse that children play on one another when left to their own devices. When he'd read *Lord of the Flies*, he'd guessed that Mr. Goldman's childhood experiences on the school playground had been the root of his pessimism. Civilization was, after all, the thinnest of veneers. But these men had never shown themselves to be pranksters; he'd never known adults who played practical jokes.

"You'll see soon enough," Johnny said.

The men melted like spectres into the shadow. Winston

stood rigid, hands balled in the pockets of his coat. Alone and literally in the dark, he felt chilled and foolish. What would Edward the Black Prince have done? He snorted aloud. Obviously, he would have never agreed to be taken anywhere; courtier heads would've rolled instead. His stomach felt queasy.

Winston could smell the mustiness of decaying leaves and the fresh sap of tree needles. The Enchanted Forest: he pictured wart-specked trolls lurking under bridges, crafty wolves, droopy-nosed dwarves in straw huts. Fair-skinned innocents waylaid by magical spells. He'd never thought about the actual Black Forest darkness of those stories; how frightened the orphaned children wandering under a sunless leafy canopy must have been. It was not fear that Winston felt now. The partial sleep and hangover had him bustling toward rancour. He was impatient for the mystery to be explained and until that happened his peering uselessly into the void made him feel as though he stood on the side of a road waiting for a bus whose schedule he did not know. Time had slowed to a crawl.

He wished that Dickie had handed over a clue about what he was supposed to be seeing or encountering in this place. Or when. Unlike the Port-Land, about which he had made suitable—if finally laughably inaccurate—conjectures, what offering a patch of forest in the middle of the November night could make to sightseers was completely puzzling. So far there was nothing noteworthy to glimpse.

Winston's mind grew fiery with images—witches at midnight covens, white slavers, Soviet agents, the Ku Klux

Klan—that he instantly extinguished. Some ideas just did not have the legs on which to stand. It would serve reason that natural phenomena such as the aurora borealis or phosphorescent sea creatures would be closer to the mark. Yet, he could not come up with a thing offhand that might show up in a forest in the middle of the night. Some nocturnal animal, perhaps? Raccoons were hardly headline news. And it seemed unlikely these men would have any abiding interest in nature. They weren't of the bird-watching sort. Delilah mocked *city slickers* for having no appreciation for the rhythms of the seasons, and would blanch if she spent an hour in the company of these gentlemen.

In the aftermath of the Judy Canova Collins, Winston's whole body registered its complaints. His thoughts turned to Alberta's detective novels and their inevitable Mickey Finns. Why would these men bother? Or might the whole clandestine undertaking be a charade, one of Dickie's odd jokes? Dickie had never shown himself to be vindictive for no cause; he seemed more bark than bite. None of it made any sense.

As his senses adjusted to the blanketing shroud of darkness, Winston heard movements and watched mobile orange orbs—lit cigarettes. He squinted, trying to make the black against black shapes coalesce. Other men came here, then; it was not a secret only the gang was privy to. Everyone followed the rule of silence. Its strict adherence, Winston thought, lent credence to his nocturnal animal theory.

A silhouette holding a glowing cigarette made its way toward Winston, its movement reminiscent of a singular though sluggish firefly. It stopped a few feet from him and drew from the cigarette. The shape moved closer until it stood next to him. Winston was frozen. A hand settled on his thigh and did not lift again. The hand squeezed gently; a moment later it crept upward, resting on the fly of his trousers. A finger dug under the flap of the fly. Winston could feel the hard edge of a fingernail run up the zipper's metal surface, the vibration an electric shock.

In a smooth, practiced movement, the shadow was crouched in front of him, the mouth directly on his trousers, the breath a sharp contrast to the autumn air. Winston's mind was stalled; he wanted to push the shape away and tear out of the bower, and yet he was curious. He was aroused. With veteran ease, the figure unhitched Winston's trousers and underpants; hands stroked his behind and a mouth— hot and soft and moist—enveloped his manhood. The sensation was like no other. Winston clutched the man's head, felt the warmth of the ears, the oiled smoothness of the hair, the prickly stubble of his beard. Breathing in the pungent tobacco smoke, he could see other figures getting closer and then fading back. The moment climaxed in no time. The figure pulled away and, like the gang minutes before him, dissipated into the forest. The night air was cold on his exposed body. Winston tucked himself into his underpants and fastened his trousers. His senses reached out as he stared with dread into the fathomless dark of the night.

## Epi[logue] I Ap[ril] [19]65

Winston lifted the squat clock that faced him from the right front corner of his desk. Winding it marked the final half hour of his working day. He also checked to see if windows were locked, made certain that no student had burrowed himself in a cubbyhole, and swept the room for leftover items that would become discards in the cardboard Lost and Found box he stored in the broom closet. Over the course of the afternoon, Winston had already picked up a white barrette, two notebooks, and a tube of lipstick. They would likely never be claimed.

He heard the library door close with a gentle click. That sound prompted his momentary frown; he foresaw having to tell this student that he'd have just five minutes before needing to leave for the day. It was an odd time for a student to show up; he should be attending some class or another. Perhaps a teacher had sent him to the library as a punishment. It was Winston's considered opinion that such a drastic measure came nowhere close to its target of correction.

A plain-looking girl with hair as black as Grendel's approached him. She held a notebook close to her bosom.

"Mr. Wilson, I'm flunking History. Can you help me?" Winston liked the gap between her front teeth.

"You have me at a disadvantage, young lady. What is your name, pray tell?"

"Em."

"Em?"

"Oh, Emily Sanderson."

"Pleased to meet you, Miss Sanderson. I don't recall having seen you in here before." He raised his eyebrows in mild castigation: *Small wonder you're failing.*

She stood in front of his desk, eyes cast downward.

"Now then, how can I be of assistance?"

"I figure that if I can do real, um, really well on the final assignment … it's worth a quarter of our final grade, you see." Winston guessed that she arrived by bus every morning from one of the outlying farms.

"Alright. What have you done so far?"

"You know that we have to write about Valley history, right?"

"Yes." He did know this topic well, Delilah Pierce's perennial final assignment, and kept folders of clippings about towns and events in the Valley in the filing cabinet next to his desk.

"Well, I thought I would do something about women in business in the early years of River Bend City. My gran says the Bend used to be run by women."

"She does, does she? That's a grand idea. But it's already fairly late in the day, Miss Sanderson. Spend a few minutes jotting down your ideas tonight and let's meet tomorrow. Will you have the spare time?"

Winston stood for a moment at the threshold of Mrs. Pierce's classroom. In her yellow dress printed with daisies, she gesticulated toward the blackboard explaining—he could hear her plain as day—the Treaties of Versailles to a small body of detainees. The instant he crowded into the edge of her vision, she turned and gave him a smile and quick wave. She returned to the after-hours remedial lecture in a beat.

He heard her skittering gait as he approached his west exit. Already guessing the urgent message she planned to deliver, he stopped and waited with a grin.

"Don't forget that you're hosting the Curriculum Committee tonight." Her bright colouration and uneasy flutter reminded Winston of a canary.

She rested her left hand over her bosom, winded from the exertion.

"Of course, Delilah. I'm not so old that I've become that forgetful. Just this morning Mother was fretting about what kind of baking she ought to serve to our little group."

"I'm sorry, Winston. Force of habit. Too many absentminded students over the years, I suppose. See you at six o'clock on the dot. Shall I bring anything?"

"Your quick wit should suffice, Delilah." Turning to the door, he adjusted his hat and pushed.

Along his route toward Wilson Manor, Winston observed the density of the heavy grey clouds and could see that yet another deluge of rain was imminent—the proper question would be "How much?" he decided resignedly, not "When?" He felt tired, under the grip of that dull weather. If he lived elsewhere, he wondered, some country with sunshine year round, would he be a more sanguine man? Not himself only, but the general population in the water-soaked Valley? Everyone here had an intimate kinship with the rainy weather blues.

And he was aware that these blues were no caprice of his. Alberta had told Winston that scientific surveys had proven that people in northern climates have a measurably greater proneness to doldrums, ruefulness, and even suicide. Maybe the life of Riley could not be found so far north. In fact, when he'd encountered the phrase *dolce far niente* in a novel about early Christian Rome it seemed felicitous, but also as exotic and beautiful as an Aegean siren—and as remote: the kind of lassitude one could achieve here for a only a few days in summer.

He couldn't remember if the crucial factor in the Nordic low mood phenomenon was abundant snowfall or lack of available light. Alberta had not mentioned rain, he was certain of that. Maybe the sheets of falling water led to a special kind of melancholic disposition and ought to be taken into account. He'd ask Cameron McKay, who kept track of that scientific sort of thing. He'd know something. At least they weren't stuck along some granite fjord in Norway. Or captive in desolate Alaska.

The Manor's front yard was full of green budding promise—for which, he grudgingly admitted, rain should be paid respect. In a matter of weeks, the shrubs and trees would be fully in leaf; day by day, the dark clusters on Alberta's white lilac trees grew plump. Their bursting forth always seemed like nature's official announcement that grey winter and its cold rains had retreated for the next half of the year.

In the front hallway he yelled out, "Hello, Mother," and checked for mail in the candy dish that had rested on the desk in the living room for as long as he could remember. No mail in hand, he headed toward the kitchen.

Alberta was scrubbing her nails under the tap. A comedy program was blaring from the radio.

She held up her dripping hands and wiggled her fingers in greeting. "It's damp out there. The dirt is chock full of worms, though. Wonderful."

Now that Winston was home, Alberta would begin with her tea preparations. She dried her hands and shuffled toward the pantry door.

While she boiled water and warmed the teapot, Winston walked to his room. He sat at the edge of his bed and removed his shoes and socks. The mismatched socks and mildly distended foot no longer drew his attention with any regular frequency. It grew on you and became part of the landscape, he'd concluded, no differently than moss on the eaves of a house. That adjustment of perspective made sense, like some purposeful vestige of the survival instinct: there was a brief time of adaptation and it transformed naturally into the way it's always been. Otherwise, the worry and anxiety would be a debilitating handicap. Forward movement and achievement of biological goals were what compelled our species, he thought. Sulking over mortality and our feeble, ever-woundable flesh was not. He wondered if the war veterans with missing limbs had similar experiences. Surely some conditions were less easy to overlook.

A passing glance at the foot now pushed up shards of memories about his black-browed specialist pressing his thumbs into the spongy skin, and, regrettably, Dickie and Errol Flynn. The scenes flashed vividly. Though he had success in keeping those few hours of his past at bay, there were moments when they flew up like furies. All he desired was that they fade away as steadily as pencil sketches. After all, he'd decided that his sense of adventure had been misguided, like that of those Bend high school students last year whose drunken inspiration to "walk the tightrope" across a narrow iron beam on the bridge had resulted in gales of tears after three young bodies had washed up miles downstream. Likewise, his participation in the incident in the city had been a grievous error.

His lapse of judgment could be overlooked—and that was something those students could never claim. With the exception of the occasional insistence of memory, the entire episode stayed securely buried. And normally there was no thumping heart under the floorboards that drove him to distraction. Why should there be? Winston knew he must learn from Pandora and Eve's fatal choices: he understood that giving into that peculiar temptation would catapult disastrous changes into his peaceful world. Why bother with it, then? Unlike his mother, he had a curiosity that was easily satisfied.

He slid on his slippers and stood up. Looking in the mirror, he saw what was always there at this hour of the weekday: a trim and well-groomed man with a full head of hair in a woollen cardigan about to share a pot of tea and a plate of biscuits with his mother.

In the kitchen, Alberta was talking back to the radio announcer. She turned off the radio as he sat at the table, pausing to breathe in the humid kitchen's comforting smoky scent.

"I stopped in and talked with Mr. Bryson today. He gave me a few new brochures." She pushed them across the table. Her excitement about their long-deferred bus tour to Nevada had grown visible as the date loomed closer. Winston looked at the tiny, inviting pictures—a cactus-shaped swimming pool, a young couple holding fancy cocktails, a stage of sequined performers, and a golden room the size of a warehouse filled with gamblers swathed in shimmering Hollywood glamour. **HIGH ROLLERS!** exclaimed the cover of another pamphlet. Winston reached down when he felt Grendel butt up against his calf.

His picture of the craggy, sun-blasted state—so tidy, pristine, and rectilinear on the map—was now overrun with frantic gamblers in man-made oases and cigarette-smoking crooners speeding through their rote-smooth patter night after night. The incongruity of the elements perplexed him. Atomic bomb test explosions and carrion birds crowded their way into his vision. He thought of the heavy grey clouds outside and scientists measuring the deleterious effects of winter weather on one's humour.

Standing at the table, Alberta was reading a brochure. "It will be such marvelous fun," she said.

"You're right, Mother, it will."

Winston watched the crows gathering on the clothesline. They were silent for the moment, but he knew that soon enough they'd begin to caw.

# Epi[logue] II Ap[ril] [19]65

Winston grabbed the squat clock that stared at him from the right front corner of his desk. As he turned its key, he wondered how many times he'd completed his working day with this ritual. And the others—he always checked to see if windows were locked, made certain that no student had borrowed himself in a cubbyhole, and swept the room for leftover items that would lay forgotten in the cardboard Lost and Found box he stored in the broom closet. Over the course of the day, Winston had already found a white barrette, two notebooks—each inscribed with teenaged proclamations of *True Love*—and a tube of lipstick. Dust would be their true love soon enough.

He heard the door close with a gentle click. The sound prompted an instantaneous frown. It irked him that it would be necessary to tell this student that he'd have just five minutes before he must leave for the day. It was an unusual time for a student to appear; he should be attending some class or another. What fool would show up so late? A delinquent, no doubt, sent to this hallowed hall of learning as some fruitless punishment.

A plain-looking girl with hair as black as Grendel's approached him. She held a notebook close to her bosom.

"Mr. Wilson, I'm flunking History. Can you help me?"

"You have me at a disadvantage, young lady. What is your name, pray tell?"

"Em."

"Em?"

"Oh, Emily Sanderson."

"Pleased to meet you, Miss Sanderson. I don't recall having seen you in here before." He raised his eyebrows. "Perhaps that may account for your less than stellar grade in History."

She stood in front of his desk, eyes cast downward.

"Now then, what are your requirements?"

"I figure that if I can do real, um, really well on the final assignment ... it's worth a quarter of our final grade, you see." Winston guessed she arrived by bus from one of the outlying farms. He admired her pluck for staying in school. Her father must be laying down the law by now, letting her know—in ways both subtle and blatant—that the farm was her rightful place and that her labour was needed there full-time. Her desire for a better life was not what mattered, she'd be told. It was the *rerum natura* for a farm girl, her father would say in so many words.

"Alright. What have you done so far?"

"You know that we have to write about Valley history, right?"

"Yes."

"Well, I thought I would do something about women in

business in the early years of River Bend City. My gran says the Bend used to be run by women."

"She does, does she? Yes, I hear a small band of Amazons settled on the riverbank decades before Father Pourguet. Look, it's already fairly late in the day, Miss Sanderson." He tapped the top of the clock with his index finger. "Spend a few minute jotting down your ideas—specific ones, not so vague—and come in with them tomorrow. Alright?"

Wandering through the library for the day's final inspection, Winston imagined Alberta as one of the lost descendants of Queen Hippolyta, bent over in her garden wearing the fabled golden girdle.

"Mr. Wilson? Oh, Mr. Wilson?"

Winston turned when he heard the fluty trill of Mrs. Pierce. She was leaning her torso into the hallway as though her dedication physically tethered her to the classroom.

"I'm done for the day, Delilah. Is there something I can help you with?"

"Oh. It's nothing. I saw you and thought you had absentmindedly forgotten to say goodbye." Her wheedling tone set his teeth on edge. It was all he could do to be pleasant. She veered between nun and spinster and neither hue in her personality held any appeal. Her coy romantic overtures were going *nowhere fast*, as Johnny would say.

"Yes, that must be it. I was … well, yes, my head was in the clouds. See you tomorrow, I suppose."

"Unless the Russians have their way. Talk to you soon!" Despite the gloomy insinuation, she waved like a schoolgirl. He pictured her writing *True Love* on her grade booklet.

Along his route toward Wilson Manor, Winston could not help but notice the density of the heavy grey clouds. There was no magic in predicting that another deluge of rain was imminent; he decided resignedly that "How much?" would be a more illuminating question than "When?" His thoughts drifted from the weather's pushiness to the invisible rays, pulses, and beams overhead. Even as he took each step, he knew, there were men living in polar isolation hundreds of miles to the north whose jobs had them monitoring machines that protected national security.

While an easy fact to forget, everyone had heard that the string of radar stations—scores of them, a marvel of science—was in constant communication as it anxiously watched the sky for airborne Soviet missiles. Winston wondered what toll the job took on the men in those frozen habitats. Facing the blasting cold, stuck in a tiny hut, and then sitting on a chair and waiting for enemy missiles to announce themselves: not the sort of work that could be described as pleasurable. Maybe the responsibility was reward enough. He guessed that drink must flow during off hours.

Their dedication was cold comfort to him. It did not offer true protection or even lull with a false sense of security. Instead, it made him believe that he was caught between the proverbial rock and a hard place, though what was Scylla and what was Charybdis remained unclear. It was all a historical accident in any case: he and his country were at the wrong place at the wrong time. While the D.E.W. Line was no folly like Maginot, Winston pictured volley after volley of missiles that would register on radar screens mere moments before they reached their targets. What use was such knowledge? There would scarcely be time for the men to reach for their telephones before the explosions started. Ordinary people would follow their routines right up until the blasts took their lives away; they'd never get word from the messengers up north.

Cameron McKay had said that protecting American leaders was the real intent behind the enterprise, and the idea was that Russian missiles would be heading to American targets—not Canadian ones—so they would fly right overhead. Yet there'd be no protection from missed targets or missiles with engines—did they have engines, Winston wondered—that stalled en route. Wedged between two bullies on a playground, the hapless child will not escape without injury. Winston thought it was an apt comparison.

The Manor's front yard was full of green budding promise—*all this juice and all this joy!*—for which, he grudgingly admitted, rain should be paid respect. In a matter of weeks the shrubs and trees would be fully in leaf; day by day, the dark clusters on Alberta's white lilac trees grew plump. Their bursting forth always seemed like nature's official announcement that grey winter and its cold rains had retreated for the next half of the year. The metamorphosis was invigorating. He recalled the old poet's sour *Earth's old glooms and pains*, but could never muster that concentration of hopelessness.

At the front door, Winston yelled out, "Hello, Mother," and walked to his bedroom. He felt eager to discard the visible signs of the day. Even in his room, the air was redolent with Alberta's Lapsang Souchung.

Once his cardigan was buttoned up and his feet were inside slippers, Winston was looking forward to tea and conversation in the kitchen's soft light.

"It's coming down in buckets," Alberta said as she was looking out the window above the sink.

"Thought I'd get caught in it." Winston picked up Grendel and cradled him upside down. The cat, he knew, would stay relaxed for well under a minute.

"You got a letter from the city."

Winston looked at her and thought he saw a trace of Delilah Pierce's pursed lips. Alberta disapproved of this friendship, he understood. They had exchanged no words over it, though she had remarked about their apparent frivolity—based solely on what he selected to tell her—and his travel extravagance more than once. She believed they ought to at least make the effort of visiting him. For Winston, their visit to the country was anathema; he did not want Dickie and Alberta to ever share tea and biscuits and idle conversation. Here was another rock and a hard place, he sighed.

Winston strode to the front hall. The envelope was from Dickie, of course—at some time he'd been voted in as the gang's official secretary of correspondence.

The note's tone was slapdash and teasing:

*April 24, 1965*

*Farmer—*

*We miss the pleasure of your company. We've discovered a new haunt, The Embassy (The Jembassy, actually, if you catch my drift). It's a stone's throw from the respectable part of town. And right next to a greaser hang out. What luck!! It's a delight, in short. We're heading out tonight.*

*Yours,*
*Dickie & Co.*

A trip to the city might be just the tonic that would fix what ailed him, he thought. Next weekend, perhaps.

"I stopped in and talked with Mr. Bryson today. He gave me a few new brochures." She slid them across the table. Her excitement about their long-deferred bus tour to Nevada had grown visible as the date loomed closer. Winston looked at the tiny, inviting pictures—a cactus-shaped swimming pool, a young couple holding fancy cocktails, a stage of sequined performers, and a golden room the size of a warehouse filled with gamblers swathed in shimmering Hollywood glamour. **HIGH ROLLERS!** exclaimed the cover of another pamphlet. Winston reached down when he felt Grendel butt up against his calf; he'd rebounded from the humiliation of not five minutes before.

His picture of the craggy, sun-blasted state—so tidy, pristine, and rectilinear on the map—was now overrun with frantic gamblers in man-made oases and cigarette-smoking crooners speeding through their rote-smooth patter night after night. The incongruity of the elements perplexed him. Atomic bomb test explosions and carrion birds crowded their way into his vision. Picturing a frost-crusted D.E.W. outpost, he guessed that the desert could also be a place where the American military kept their arsenal of missiles stored away. No one would suspect a thing. It was the middle of nowhere; one might hide a whole fleet of B-52 bombers there with no fear of being found out.

Standing at the table, Alberta was reading a brochure. "It will be such marvelous fun," she said.

Winston wondered whether any of the gang—Johnny, most probably—might know of any special places he might visit while there. There must be some cocktail lounge. Alberta would want to spend one or two afternoons gambling. He'd oblige her and find something else to occupy his time.

"You're right, Mother, it will," he said.

Winston watched the crows gathering on the clothesline. They were silent for the moment, but he knew that soon enough they'd begin to caw.

Appendix I:

The *Reeves Business College Guide to Beauty • Charm • Poise*
archive

The local surfacing of the foregoing narrative's manuscript was a fortuitous accident. A detailed account of its discovery within a 1958 high school Home Economics manual entitled *Junior Homemaking* can be found in Afterword (An Introduction), page 216. Literally bound to that Home Economics textbook with elastic bands, another quaint tome, the *Reeves Business College Guide to Beauty • Charm • Poise*, divulged two germane varieties of artifact that had been stowed away between its pages.

The first (see Appendix II: "Obscenity," page 207) is an eight-page scene that features Dickie, Ed, and Johnny; if inserted into the principal narrative it would logically follow the dinner at the Bamboo Terrace sequence in "J[une 19]59." The complete absence of Winston from the scene—which would be the sole instance in the story—offers one plausible explanation for its physical exclusion from the *Junior Homemaking cachette*. Another possibility, as the manuscript's scrawled title hints, relates to the scene's frank discussion of sexual intercourse. Such explicit description would simply not have been publishable in its day; nor does its coarseness accord, *sensu stricto*, with the tone of the larger manuscript.

The second lot of material, an assortment of five histor-ical artifacts, is intriguing insofar as three of the documents are named explicitly during Winston's appearance at the curriculum planning committee's meeting at the conclusion of "A[pril 19]59"; Dickie's invitation to his "Errol Flung!" masquerade in "O[ctober 19]59" replicates the headline of the fourth. Such source material furnishes clues about the cultural currents that the author aimed to synthesize into the novel's pages, making a direct correlation between the novel's setting and the historical reality of the author's era. The final artifact, a flattened canister of Malkin's brand mace, confirms the historical veracity of Dot West and is, moreover, suggestive of a linkage between the author and the world of advertising represented by Johnny Schmidt.

—A.X.P.

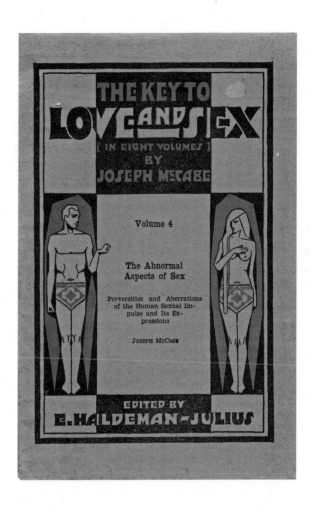

Figure 1a.
Cover
*The Keys to Love and Sex (in Eight Volumes):*
*Volume 4: The Abnormal Aspects of Sex*
by Joseph McCabe, edited by E. Haldeman-Julius
(Girard, Kansas: Haldeman-Julius Publications, n.d.)

CONTENTS

Page

Chapter I. Abnormal Sex-Life Amongst Savages.......... 5

(1) Why It Is Comparatively Rare. (2) Abnormal Conduct.

Chapter II. Abnormal Sex-Life in the Ancient Civilizations.........11

(1) In Ancient Times. (2) Other Abnormalities.

Chapter III. The Scientific Study of Abnormalities..........17

(1) Pre-Scientific Literature About Sex. (2) Medical Study in the Nineteenth Century. (3) The Modern Psychology of Sex.

Chapter IV. The Practice of Masturbation..........24

(1) Extent of the Practice. (2) Modern Views of the Effect.

Chapter V. Erotic Symbolism and Other Phenomena..........27

(1) Sexual Fetishism. (2) Exhibitionism.

Chapter VI. Sadism and Masochism..........29

(1) The Modern Study of Sadism. (2) Flagellation. (3) Masochism.

Chapter VII. The Homosexual Impulse..........37

(1) The Homosexual Temperament. (2) Modern Views. (3) Homosexuals and the Law.

Chapter VIII. Sex and Insanity..........43

Figure 1b.
Table of Contents
*The Keys to Love and Sex (in Eight Volumes):*
*Volume 4: The Abnormal Aspects of Sex*
by Joseph McCabe, edited by E. Haldeman-Julius
(Girard, Kansas: Haldeman-Julius Publications, n.d.)

uncertainty about matters of health, a prompt talk with a good physician is the quickest way out of trouble.

*Homosexuality.* Like everything else in the human mind and body, the sexual instincts sometimes go wrong. There are men who are attracted sexually by other men or boys. This disturbance may be a deep-seated trait, or it may be acquired under special circumstances and may be temporary, even alternating with more normal sex interests.

In young children mere curiosity about the sex organs may lead to sex play between two children of the same sex. This is of course not a serious matter. Boys who are maturing sexually, at the age of thirteen or fourteen and up, sometimes go beyond mere sex play and handling of the genitals, into definite homosexual excitement. This too is generally a temporary kind of behavior and there is no reason for feelings of deep guilt about it, though it had better be avoided. Confirmed homosexuality in grown boys and men is a different matter. In the first place the very

75

thought of homosexuality is disagreeable to men who do not have such impulses. They feel unconsciously that it is useless biologically and therefore unnatural. In the second place homosexual experiences may make people less susceptible to the attractions of the opposite sex and thus less likely to marry; or if they do marry their capacity for normal sex life, upon which domestic happiness partially depends, may be limited. Homosexual friendships are characteristically stormy and troublesome. In the lower levels of the community criminal conduct tends to center around homosexual groups, and the homosexual individual may become the victim of blackmail or may otherwise suffer from difficulties associated with his sex habits. It must be clearly understood, however, that there are also homosexual men of good education and high general character who are able to control their tendency and keep it from disturbing their usefulness. Treatment by a physician skilled in mental guidance may cure the aberration. Contrary to a widespread im-

76

Figure 2.

'Homosexuality'

From Chapter VII, "Sex Disorders."

In *Attaining Manhood: A Doctor Talks to Boys About Sex Second Edition, Revised and Enlarged* by George W. Corner, M.D.

(New York: Harper and Row, 1952: 75, 76)

IS AN 'IRRESISTIBLE URGE' AN ACCEPTABLE EXCUSE?

*Earl Jowitt:* I do not accept for one moment the doctrine of the irresistible impulse. The psychologists have told me that they are quite unable at present to distinguish between an impulse which is irresistible and an impulse which has not been resisted. I hope we shall hear nothing more about this. I suppose it is a fact that these unhappy people have temptations of a nature or kind which do not attack the ordinary man. But the ordinary man has his temptations, too, and he has to learn to resist his temptations. So it seems to me that the people who are cursed in this way must also resist their temptations. That is the least we can expect of them.

*Earl Winterton:* I suppose the advocates of change would regard as the strongest argument of all, what I would describe as the 'irresistible

Figure 3.
'Is an "irresistible urge" an acceptable excuse?'
Detail from "Appendix One: Abstracts From the House of Lords Debate 19th May, 1954."
In *They Stand Apart: A Critical Survey of the Problem of Homosexuality*
edited by His Honour Judge Tudor Rees and Harley V. Usill (London: William Heinemann, 1955: 202)

Figure 4.
"Actor Dies in Vancouver Suite"
by Jack Wasserman, *The Sun*, final edition,
Thursday October 15, 1959: A1

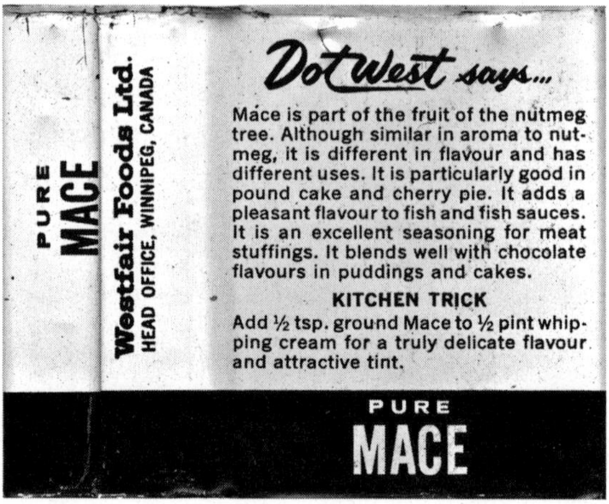

PURE
MACE

Westfair Foods Ltd.
HEAD OFFICE, WINNIPEG, CANADA

*Dot West says...*

Mace is part of the fruit of the nutmeg tree. Although similar in aroma to nutmeg, it is different in flavour and has different uses. It is particularly good in pound cake and cherry pie. It adds a pleasant flavour to fish and fish sauces. It is an excellent seasoning for meat stuffings. It blends well with chocolate flavours in puddings and cakes.

**KITCHEN TRICK**

Add ½ tsp. ground Mace to ½ pint whipping cream for a truly delicate flavour and attractive tint.

PURE
MACE

Figure 5.
"Dot West says…"
Pure Mace canister
Westfair Foods Ltd
Head Office, Winnipeg, Canada

Johnny stood behind the bar, all the while complaining in a low voice. Mixology was an art, he repeated, requiring an intuitive eye. The best bartender is no scientist stirring a beaker with his nose in a book. "Come and taste," he commanded, and offered Ed the completed cocktail, his palm flattened into a serving tray. "It's no science, I tell you. You either have a feel for it or you don't."

"Hmmm," Ed replied, swishing the liquid from cheek to cheek. "A bit sweet, actually. If only you'd used the jigger...."

"Why don't you two give it a rest," Dickie said with a tremulous voice, reclining on the armchair, legs crossed. "You know, I'm feeling a wee bit misty-eyed. The shenanigans between your nubile *nephew*—and just what possessed you to pull that fib out of the air?—and that busty thing a table over tonight got me to thinking about young love. It's been ages, I know, but I used to be a bright young lad, chock full of 'will you be my valentine?'"

He made his way to the mirror and leaned in closely. "You'd never guess it now, would you? I see a veritable stampede of crow's feet before me."

"You're glorious, Miss Desmond," Johnny said from the bar.

"What about you two? Were you once fresh-cheeked maidens with delicate pink hearts all aflutter?"

"Is it true love you're speaking of or merely the beast with two backs?" Johnny asked. He squeezed a lemon wedge with a flourish.

"Let me see. Now that you've given me a choice, I say a plain old groping with the lights out story might liven us up a bit. Things have become a *un peu grave* since we left the Farmer at Bamboo Terrace."

"You first, then." Cocktail tray in hand he walked over to Dickie and then onward to the chesterfield. "Scoot over," he said to Ed.

"I suppose you both know of the Captain and the Contessa? Well, my story is nowhere near so sublime. After I finished high school, I worked in the Shoe Department at Fields. It was okay. Anyway, one day a businessman—who shall remain nameless—came over." Dickie strode away from the mirror at a purposeful pace and sat at the edge of the coffee table.

"He tried on pair after pair, all the while giving me the eye and asking questions about school, girls, what I planned to do with myself, and so on. When no one was around, he clasped my hand and placed it smack dab on his thigh. I could feel the heat right through his trousers. Then, in an everyday voice, he announced he'd come back at closing time. He left without even buying polish!

"When closing time rolled around, he hadn't returned. I

was such a naïve thing!" He drew from his cocktail for a moment. "I had absolutely no idea what he had planned. The actual physical part, if you know what I mean. Back then I didn't know an iota about Greek this or French that. Why would I? Well, I had seen writing on the wall, but that's another story. Anyway, all the day, I imagined us kissing, but when I tried to picture what would happen after that, my imagination failed me. Completely. When he didn't show, I felt a bit miffed because it was an exciting prospect. Of course, nothing like that had ever happened to me before, so naturally I was on tenterhooks.

"I left Fields with a glum face, but the man was sitting behind the wheel of his car. He waved me over and asked me if I wanted to take a ride with him. Once inside he directed my hand right to his lap again, but this time I could feel more than heat. Quite a lot more. I'd have had to be daft to miss it. Like a cucumber, I tell you." He placed his drink on the table and raised his hands to measure, fisherman-style.

"Oh boy, that's big alright." Ed raised his eyebrows.

"When I got home my mother asked where I traipsed off to after work. She was happy to hear that I'd gone out with friends from Fields. Her little Richie was fitting in!" He stood up and walked toward the balcony door. Rain was pouring in sheets.

"Well, it's not a romantic story, but there you have it. You know, we went for drives for about a year. For some reason he'd always bring me donuts, a boxed baker's dozen each time.... It was hell on the figure, I tell you, but I didn't think it would be polite to refuse them. His wife must have suspected something. The poor idiot bought them from the bakery where she worked."

"Very nice, Dickie. Now come back over here and make yourself comfortable. It must have been quite an education he gave you. Alright then, I have two stories, one bent and one straight," Johnny said with a smirk.

"I don't want to hear a fishy tale," Dickie grimaced.

"Both?" Ed asked.

"Another time."

"Okay, here goes. The place: flat and ugly Flin Flon, industrial heart of northern Manitoba. The date: the last day of the blistering summer of 1937. War was in the air and my only dream was to get out of that backward mining town any way I could."

"Oh, the drama!" Dickie was smiling.

"Like dearest Dickie, I was slaving away selling shoes and shirts to the wives of working stiffs. It was lousy, but it was either MacLeods Mercantile or in the copper pits with every other schmo. Those men looked old, I tell you, even when they were twenty-one. Poor Frankie would be stooped and weathered like a grandfather by now. We'd be beyond the pale, needless to say."

"Anyway, Saint Johnny. Enough with the bleeding heart."

"You've got the patience of a bird!" he said, glaring at Dickie. "'I stuck it in him.' There you go. End of story. Satisfied?" He reached into his shirt pocket for matches.

"C'mon," Ed said, interrupting the silence.

"Only if Impatient Griselda over there behaves herself."

"Yes, ok, very well," Dickie said, crossing his legs.

"I wasn't too close to anyone," Johnny said. He slowly stirred his drink with his finger. "I think I was a wee bit obnoxious in those days because I was forever carrying on about Madison Avenue and the Big Life. If I met someone like my younger self right now I'd think he was a pompous fool. Give him a little smack and take him down a notch.

"Anyway"—Johnny swallowed the last if his cocktail— "There was another boy, a carrot-top also named John, who planned on getting to Europe. He joined the army in hopes of making it there sooner than later … and I suppose he did, and stayed there too, six feet under in Belgium.

"We knew each other well enough to nod a hello and to pass the time. He came into the store one day with an envelope in his hand. 'I'm gonna get there, I know it' he said, and showed me the letter from the Department of Defense.

"I was proud of his escape and not a little envious. When he invited me to come to his house, I accepted, even though I'd never been there before. He lived with his parents still. I figured he was just celebrating his victory and wanted anyone—including myself—along for the ride."

He paused and stubbed out his cigarette. "Gee, it's coming down in buckets," Ed exclaimed, face slanting upward to the ceiling.

"So when I got there his mother answered the door. I introduced myself and she said they were expecting me. She led me to the living room. His dad and two sisters were there, the father telling his son about his time in the trenches. Afterwards, when I thought about it, I guessed the joviality was forced. They'd stationed his father in France during the Great War, after all, so everyone knew that going to Europe would not mean only sunsets on the Seine."

Dickie cleared his throat loudly twice and checked his watch.

"Okay, okay," Johnny continued. "We sat around for a while. John's father offered us some beer, which we accepted like it was an everyday event. Not too much later we headed upstairs to John's bedroom. It was his mother's suggestion. 'I'll bet you two want to talk on your own,' she'd chimed. Up there he told me he'd always thought we were quite alike and I guessed that he meant we both wanted to get out of Flin Flon. Nope.

"He put his finger to his lips for a sec, then kept talking about Parisian this and that, then put his ear to the door. He was painting a picture with his words, but eventually—just like Dickie's mystery beau—he grabbed my hand and placed it fly level on his trousers. Then he sat right next to me and ran his hands along my shirt toward the waist. He unbuckled my pants. I just sat there witless."

Johnny stopped and looked from Ed to Dickie. "Another round, gentlemen?" he asked with the hint of a smile.

"I can wait," Ed said.

"So can I, till you finish your story at least," Dickie said.

"Okay, so in about ten seconds flat, he had my pants at my knees and his around his ankles. He sat directly on me. I slid in. Just like that. All the time he was downstairs with his family, he had been greased up and planning to take it from me. With him bouncing up and down like a fiend—a very quiet one, mind you—I lasted all of a minute.

"He must have done that all a time or two before. With whom, I could never fathom. It did give me pause, though, a fresh perspective on Flin Flon's twilight society. He was like a pro. I'm not exactly bantam weight, as you might have heard on the grapevine."

"Or read on the men's room wall," Ed said.

"Of course, Johnny. You're a giant amongst men." Dickie rolled his eyes.

"And, of course, I never had a chance to ask. I didn't see him again after that night."

"He didn't waste any time, did he, right down to business?" Dickie asked. "The donut man kept my face muffled in his lap for the whole year. We never did anything else. Not even a kiss."

"Edwina? It's your turn," Dickie said.

"Well, you know that I grew up just south of Calgary, right?" Ed said. "We'd hire guys around harvest time. His name was Bran."

"Bran?" Dickie squealed. "You have got to be kidding. Are you sure it wasn't 'Husk' or maybe 'Chaff'?"

"Be nice, Dickie. We didn't make fun of your Mr. Donut," Johnny said.

"Very well. Fix us another round, perhaps? It'll calm my frayed nerves." Dickie tilted his empty glass back and forth with mock insistence.

"Ed?" Johnny was already on his way to the bar.

"Please. Just a smidgen less sweet this time."

Johnny stuck out his tongue in reply.

"Would you mind if I fixed us a snack, Dickie, some crackers and cheese?" Ed asked. "I'm peckish. You know what they say about Chinese food."

"Help yourself," Dickie said. "There are some dill pickles too. Check the refrigerator."

The sudden bustle silenced the rain that had been loudly announcing its arrival through the ceiling.

Ed returned with a stack of side plates and an oval platter strewn with crackers, a mound of cubed cheddar, and sliced pickles. Johnny distributed cocktails.

"You weren't exaggerating when you said you were hungry again. Now, let's get back to your story," said Dickie.

"Alright, just give me a minute to fix these for us." With toothpicks he stabbed cheese, then pickle, and settled the pairing on crackers. The men devoured their midnight snack.

"Let me see, now. To be honest, what I remember the most was, um, he had an unusual smell. Reminded me of hay, but sweet too, like fresh grass. I'm not kidding. And soft hair the colour of honey. He was a talker, big plans for himself. One day he invited me to come into the barn."

"Where else!" Dickie snorted.

"We stretched out on some hay bales and he told me that one day soon he was going to drive from sea to sea to sea. He wanted to make it to New Orleans eventually. It was right at sunset, and the light made him look like an angel."

"He was a couple years older than me, maybe twenty-one. I'd never given a thought to being anywhere but on the farm, so I have him to thank for that."

"Well?" Dickie asked.

"Oh, right. He was telling me about surfing in California that day, and he said that a man could find paradise there. Then, just like that, he flipped open his overalls, pulled up his shirt, and played with himself with his eyes closed, talking about pretty girls in bikinis dancing at beach parties."

"What did you do, Ed?" Johnny asked.

"I watched till he finished. I suppose that he expected me to grab him or help him out or something, but I was too timid."

"Hmmm. I don't think that counts," Dickie decided.

"I concur," Johnny said.

"Oh, really? Then I have to skip forward a few more years. My first day here: the train station men's room. It was nothing special, but, boy, at the time it was heaven. That old fellow knew a thing or two!"

"Ah, yes, that terminus," Johnny said. "A place, I've no doubt, where many a boy has become a man. Maybe some Indian tribe made it a place for a sacred fertility ritual centuries back. There's got to be some reason for its popularity."

"Well, Johnny, it is the major departure and arrival point," Ed said with no little sarcasm.

Dickie stood up. "Another time, gentlemen." He picked up the side plates. "At the risk of offending your tender sensibilities, I'm going to close up shop for the day. I have an engagement in the morning, unlike some of you."

## Afterword (An Introduction)

## by A.X. Palios

Then there is the catch: where does justification end and degeneracy begin? Society must condemn to protect. Permit even the intellectual homosexual a place of respect and the first bar is down. Then comes the next and the next until the sadist, the flagellist [sic], the criminally insane demand their places, and society ceases to exist. So I ask again: where is the line drawn? Where does degeneracy begin if not at the beginning of individual freedom in such matters?

—James Barr, *Quatrefoil* (1950)

Allowing same sex marriage will affect the society. New trends will be set which will not be desirable. Marriage benefits would have to be provided to them as well and a new air of freedom will be provided where all sorts of crazy behaviours might be expected, adaptation to which will be almost impossible.

—Letter to the editor, *National Post* (2005)

An enigmatic phenomenon with a rareness that rivals emeralds, the literary *objet trouvé*—whether the Dead Sea Scrolls or Heinrich Böll's *The Silent Angel*—possesses a mystique borne of its very obscurity. Unearthed after being waylaid for eons in an arid cave or long forgotten in a trunk lodged in the attic of the author's remote ancestor, the manuscript is radiant with the secrets its fragile pages have sequestered. "I hold great knowledge," those pages whisper with the otherworldly gravitas of an ancient sibyl.

In our era, it is virtually only the lost manuscripts of canonical artists (Hemingway's *The Garden of Eden*, for instance, or a newly recovered Beethoven symphonic score) that are judged publishable by the vested interests that guide university presses and commercial houses. The foregoing "novel" has an exceptional status, then, insofar as it appears with no pedigree, no oeuvre, and indeed no name appended to it at all. The work's anonymity guarantees its status as *sui generis*. The manuscript can reveal nothing about the overall nature of the author's work because, of course, it has no claimant. Thus, if the editor's principal rationale for publishing a newfound manuscript relates to edification—its shedding further light on (and so ameliorating the fragmentary understanding of) the literary figure—and the marketer's impetus stems from assurances of a secure audience (those interested in the literature as well as those entranced by the celebrity of the charismatic author), then there is no conventional justification for bringing under public scrutiny the never-told tale of fictional Mr. Winston Wilson, resident of fictional River Bend City, British Columbia, Canada.

No trifling literary curiosity, though, this long-shrouded volume performs invaluable services. For the curious soul, it encourages questions about its very nature: "What is it, who wrote it, and why was it hidden away?" And its pages act as goads, urging a closer examination of the culture by which its author was enveloped. Uniquely positioned as a particularly talkative historical artifact, moreover, the manuscript also incites the inquisitive reader to grow introspective and to speculate about how extensively national culture has transformed and progressed over the last half-century. Or, indeed, the cynic with an awareness of the 1996 Republican-sponsored, Democratic President-authorized Defense of Marriage Act and recent distraught politicking in Canada about same-sex unions might hypothesize that this ostensible progress has in fact been sluggish, uncertain, and by no means assured.

Though the manuscript bears witness to a discrete historical moment, that era is not so distant as to be unrecognizable. To my long-observant eyes—on the frigid November night that Winston Wilson is led into the "enchanted forest" of the manuscript, I was a nine-year-old innocent in Manchester; and such autobiographic candor here merely highlights the fact that I have endured several feast and famine decades of so-called gay liberation—these pages expose an archetypal conflicted authorial preoccupation that to a large degree results from rigid (if not wholly stifling) and profoundly intrusive social institutions. The narrative reflects the dilemma of a character whose emergent sexuality is an unwelcome surprise because its visibility will cause him profound distress, placing the newly criminalized man in direct opposition to the terra firma of his homeland. This protagonist quite understandably intuits that if chosen, his transition from comforting normalcy to the aberrant and completely unfamiliar fringe will be accompanied with great pain. The manuscript's epilogues illustrate the conservatism of his eventual choice(s). Eerily, as a historical artifact, the manuscript appears to echo the story it tells, since the person who wrote what amounts to a gay *Bildüngsroman* either circulated it privately or else decided that circa 1959 Canadian society (or the Canadian publishing industry) was not hospitable to his perspective. Before proceeding with a tentative assessment of the revelations of this local if "lost" author, however, it seems appropriate to begin with the tale of its serendipitous discovery.

At the beginning of the 2002 autumn semester, a former student[1] appeared at my office door holding an indigo plastic bag from The Gap; here, apparently, was the "find" about which he had sent me an email a few weeks earlier. Just returned to campus from his family's home in the Fraser Valley's suburban sprawl (where he had taken a summer job at an American retail giant located in some massive consumption/entertainment complex), his eagerness to bring in an object—one that he had promised me was "really cool"—beamed from his face. In his email of mid-August he had explained that while exploring a collectibles shop, Tina's Trash & Treasures, one afternoon, two peculiar vol-

---

1. Gratitude must be expressed to "hexman35." For reasons known only to himself, my former student wishes to be acknowledged by his Internet pseudonym.

umes bound by elastic bands in the pell-mell piles of faded Tupperware, chipped porcelain figurines, and miscellaneous ersatz antiquities had caught his eye. He'd also said that he planned for me to wait until his return to campus before I could physically see what was so interesting about these mysterious publications. Since students commonly have an odd yet ardent belief that any book older than themselves is a relic worth its weight in gold, I presumed his treasure would be at best nothing other than a dusty first edition.

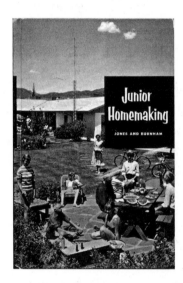 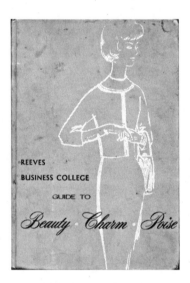

Figure 1
*Junior Homemaking* and *Reeves Business College Guide to Beauty • Charm • Poise*

It was this prize that he had now carried across campus for my bibliophilic eyes to peruse. Removing the bulky material from the bag, he snapped off the elastic bands that kept the shape intact. He placed two hardcover books on my desk. They were mid-twentieth-century, kitschy tomes that would amuse, inspire, and appall feminists and scholars of gender: a high school Home Economics textbook titled *Junior Homemaking*,[2] and *Reeves Business College Guide to Beauty • Charm • Poise*,[3] the etiquette manual for a formerly august, now defunct institution in Lloydminster, Saskatchewan that promised to transform ill-mannered adolescent females into elegant young ladies. He opened the front cover of the textbook and slowly turned the preliminary pages. The volume did not contain the expected series of chapters, however. My student revealed a hollow core: a secretive or anxious soul had dedicated an afternoon to cutting out a cradle in which to rest a prized fetish object. One might easily imagine a penitentiary inmate or a privacy-obsessed teen proceeding with such a compulsive undertaking. Yet to our eyes, this *cachette* held nothing resembling contraband; it was tightly stacked with bundles of not even yellowed paper.

"It's somebody's story," said the volume's erstwhile guardian.

My student explained that though he had dislodged

2. It *is* a first edition, but the 1958 home economics textbook authored by Evelyn G. Jones and Helen A. Burnham (of the Denver Public Schools Department) and published by the J.B. Lippincott Company of Chicago, is neither rare nor of much market value. Likewise, the *Reeves Business College Guide to Beauty • Charm • Poise* (published by Milady Publications of New York City in 1955) possesses value only as a curio.

3. See the appendices for the contents of the second book. While the sheaves were written by the same hand and the story they relate involves three of the manuscript's principle characters, . the evidence that these pages are not meant as part of the narrative in the *Junior Homemaking* *cachette* is overwhelming. The fact that they were placed in a separate volume and have been characterized by the apparent author as "Obscenity" is already amply conclusive. Moreover, there are no scenes in *The Age of Cities* in which the protagonist Winston Wilson is absent. The pages found in *Reeves Business College Guide to Beauty • Charm • Poise* portray a scene that takes place once Winston has left the scene.

the first few sheets and read them, he had left the rest of the artifact intact. Thank the gods for small mercies: he told me that when he is not rummaging like a scavenger through used goods shops, he's an adherent of crime dramas on television—and on these programs the forensics teams are adamant that the crime scene be given a *cordon sanitaire* until after their investigation has terminated. Otherwise, he elaborated, "the evidence could become tainted." I had been promoted to Textual Forensics Expert, I could see. An enthusiastic amateur hoping to solve the mystery of the book's origin, he had diligently returned to the shop in order to quiz the proprietor. She was unhelpful, the student informed me. Her reply? Wearing a sheepish look, he recalled that the gravel-voiced merchant had been succinct to the point of bluntness: "Don't ask me, honey. We get a shitload of books in here every damned week." Thus concluded one promising line of inquiry.

Figure 2
The *Junior Homemaking cachette*

He left his untitled[4] "find" with me. The temptation to read the contents was not to be resisted. Yet before giving into that first bibliophilic impulse, I thought to be methodical; each one of the tightly-bound sheaves, accordingly, was labeled and catalogued. It was scarcely necessary. The obscure author who had placed the sheaves of papers inside must have been nothing if not cautious and precise. Each "page," a piece of paper exactly 20.3 cm wide and 15.25 cm long (but folded in half lengthwise), was numbered and placed atop the next. With the exception of one untitled sheet inscribed with epigraph-like excerpts of poems by Virgil and Edgar Lee Masters, sections had been labeled "Prol S 58," "A 59," "J 59," "O 59," and so on, and then tied together with cotton twine and arranged by narrative chronology in the *cachette*. Every sentence, moreover, had been written with a soft lead pencil (all the better to correct errors?); the author had made use of just one side of each sheaf.

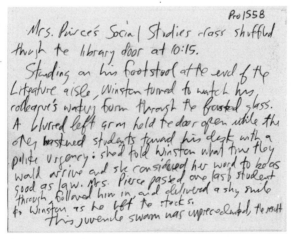

Figure 3
Manuscript page "Prol S 58"

Unlike the famously haphazard collected poems of Emily Dickinson or the equally notorious illegible manuscripts of Charlotte Brontë, both the order and clarity of these manuscript pages presented no impediments; there was no ambiguity to be found, no word undecipherable, no sheaf improperly ordered. Transcription proceeded without incident. The flawless legibility hinted that this manuscript was less a work-in-progress than a completed draft.[5]

Now that the manuscript had seen the light of day, the question of what to do with it arose as a matter of course. There was little appeal in keeping it stored away in my office as though it were mine alone to possess. The manuscript was in fact valuable as a revelatory historical document—its narrative pointedly set between the historically-veracious hanging of a homosexual murderer in spring and the death of a bisexual matinee idol in autumn—that provides certain access to a subjectivity and a subculture entirely invisible to the popular imagination. Furthermore, the manuscript's cultural portrait both complicates and localizes the understanding of a bygone era grossly simplified and homogenized by influential American media images (from exer-

4. In search of a prompt from the text, I discovered the single circumstance of words circled in pencil, apparently by the author. In the manuscript's second chapter, "J[une 19]59," Alberta envisions the Fraser delta "before the age of cities." The final four words are heavily circled in the manuscript.

5. Then again, there is evidence to support another interpretation. There's the uncharacteristic brevity of the work to consider as well as the absence of elements that typically accompany a realist narrative (a detailed history of incidents from the childhood and adolescence of the central characters, for example). While somewhat reminiscent of the conclusion of Nathanael West's Hollywood exposé, *The Day of the Locust* (1939), the sudden appearance of "choppy" episodic scenes toward the close of the final chapter are suggestive of an incomplete (if near to being whole) novel.

cises in exclusively heterosexual nostalgia such as *American Graffiti, Grease,* and *Happy Days* to a trapped-in-amber syndicated series like *Leave It to Beaver*).

Seeking the publication of an anonymous work was unusual, admittedly, but there were literary elements to it as well that recommended I introduce it to other readers. Yet, in assessing the merit of the volume for publication purposes, the question of authorship remained a troubling—and by no means trivial—detail. It seemed imperative to solve the mystery and reveal the source. Despite my best efforts, that quest was fruitless. No inner Hercule Poirot could I make manifest; evidence was sullen, revealing no secrets. Avenues proposed by colleagues proved unproductive as well.

Necessity was in fact the mother of invention in this case, and for me inventiveness entailed contacting graphologists and text authenticators. This extraordinary—one might say desperate—measure reflected my native skepticism being overwhelmed by frustration. I did, incidentally, draw the line at a recommended "forensic psychic" who promises to reveal truth upon laying her hands on any artifact. While graphology has always shined like a dubious beacon of pseudo-science for me (like phrenologists, television psychics, and readers of tea leaves: a trap for the credulous), I decided nevertheless to send copies of the same two manuscript pages to a pair of respected graphologists, one in Ontario and the other in Oklahoma.[6] "What's the harm?" I conclud-

6. Derrill Dobkins, Certified Graphologist, was the past president of the Ontario Chapter of the International Graphoanalyst Society. He graciously offered me the number of an American counterpart, Marlyse Winterbourne of Enid, Oklahoma, whose experience with police investigations is, Dobkins said, the stuff of IGS legend.

ed, borrowing some of Winston Wilson's late-blooming devil-may-care attitude.

Regrettably, their results were mere sketches and, accordingly, inconclusive. Each employed their specialist's vocabulary of inflated buckles, open loops, hooks, strokes, degree of connection, upstrokes, sloping t-bars, and line spacing, but their analyses could not supply much concrete data. The Canadian analyst, for instance, detected "literary leanings," "pessimism," "repression," "consistency," "desire for change," and "caution" in the handwriting of the unknown author. From the same sample, the Oklahoman deduced "caution" and "repression." She determined additional traits: "sarcasm," "idiosyncrasy," "narrow-mindedness," and "indecisiveness." The composite personality that results brings us nowhere close to a useful (or even coherent) profile. The best efforts of these experts could not ultimately coax the now schizoid but still ghostly author from "the other side." Interestingly, both analysts ascertained that the writer was a left-handed male, and Ms. Winterbourne supplemented her assertion with a curious and terse notation: "May have issues about his masculinity." The analysts of paper and ink could confirm that the text was produced between 1955 and 1965. The quality of the products was not exceptional. Their commonplace nature effectively prevented the extraction of any further information[7] that might reveal the absent author.

---

7. The last, truly desperate measure was a weekend trip to Tina's Trash & Treasures. The coarse woman my student had described proved unhelpful yet again. She could not recall the specific volume, nor give me an estimate of the point of origin for the boxes of books in which it had be found. She did inform me that her "scrounger" traveled throughout the Valley and spent weekends in Vancouver flea markets. In short, the book could have come from an estate sale in tony Point Grey or a swap meet held at a farm in Matsqui.

If the mystery of authorship remains—permanently?—unresolved (or else we heed Michel Foucault's warning that our quest for the inviolable origin of things is an understandable if wrong-headed and quite possibly foolhardy venture[8]), a secondary mystery is surely worth our consideration: why had this manuscript been sequestered away? If it was autobiographical or a *roman à clef*, then it is sensible to assume that the author would not dare risk the public exposure (humiliation or retribution) that publication would be sure to bring. Another possibility, equally probable, is that a second copy of the manuscript was actually sent out for publication and subsequently rejected. Since publishers do not maintain records (or an archive) of rejected manuscripts, verification of any sort is not forthcoming yet again.

Granting the complete absence of the author and knowledge about "his" social circumstances, it is intriguing to speculate further on the author's historical predicament. A cursory overview of the Canadian literary infrastructure indicates that while there is undoubtedly such an animal today—a thriving one supported by government grants, televised awards ceremonies, arts festivals, university English departments, agents, and so forth—it was still fundamentally inchoate circa 1959 and, then as now, based largely in Toronto. Moreover, that miniscule publishing sector's interest in the literary vanguard is undetectable. Seeing that an American author like William Burroughs was publishing such risqué works as *Junkie* (1953) and *Naked Lunch* (1959) during the period, it does not seem reckless to contend

---

8. "Nietzsche, Genealogy, History" in *Language, Counter-Memory, Practice*: 148.

that Canadian publishing house concerns invested heavily in conventional literary stock. In short, at mid-century (an age well before the foreign-owned multinational publishing conglomerates of today) Canada was no haven for the publication of a novice writer on the edge of the nation holding what would have amounted to a radically controversial perspective.

Nor did publishers print as many titles as today. Surveying literary production between 1940 and 1960 in a 1965 essay, Hugo McPherson reports that some 370 literary novels were published in Canada during the period (a staggering 1.5 per month, in other words), the bulk of which, he states, "consist[ed] of domestic romances, often honest or earnest in intention, but abjectly imitative of the stereotypes of magazine fiction."[9] McPherson complains that this Canadian fiction had all the hallmarks of provincialism since its choice of material was decidedly unworldly and apolitical. (Similarly, discussing the literature of social protest and social change during the same period, W.H. New[10] makes mention of novels and poems addressing voting rights, living wages, and labour unrest. The politics of gender, sexuality, and skin colour were to rear their heads a full decade later.) McPherson's essay bluntly includes a long statement by one J.R. MacGillivray, whose unequivocal conclusion (in 1949) was that Canadian novelists have "no apparent awareness of ideas and events, but [live in] a perfect isolation from place and time." MacGillivray then exposed his profound

9. "Fiction (1940-1960)" in *Literary History of Canada*: 207.

10. *A History of Canadian Literature*: 150-156.

disappointment with a rhetorical question: "Where else is there the equal to that ivory tower, soundproof, windowless, air-conditioned, and bombproof, in which these novelists tap at their typewriters undisturbed by the falling heavens?"[11] If in general literature of the era was a parochial, apolitical, and timid family, we can surmise that it would not have welcomed a shameful cousin like Winston Wilson and his unrepentant homosexual comrades into its fold with open arms. It would seem likely that something as trifling as Alberta's sympathetic response to Leo Mantha (the scandalous *amour fou* murderer, an inmate at the Fraser Valley's Oakalla Prison Farm, and, on April 28, 1959, the last man put to death by hanging in British Columbia) might have prompted a censorious reply.

McPherson does eventually submit a list comprised of a "small group of writers who in various ways have expanded the Canadian consciousness of the self, and its relation to ideas, imagination, and events."[12] That group includes Hugh MacLennan, Barry Callaghan, Gabrielle Roy, Robertson Davies, Sinclair Ross, Ethel Wilson, and Mordecai Richler. It is a minute canon of figures, we might add, whose representation of Canada (and whose influential contributions to "the Canadian consciousness of the self") is stocked exclusively with heterosexual characters and predicaments. Tradition-minded literary vision aside, there is no doubting that the St. Laurent/Diefenbaker years were also a time of literary-cultural expansion, a fact made espe-

11. "Fiction (1940-1960)" in *Literary History of Canada*: 207.

12. Ibid: 210.

cially clear by the growth of literary journals—like *Contact* (1952), *Tamarack Review* (1956), *Waterloo Review* (1958), *Canadian Literature* (1959), *Prism* (1959), and *Tish* (1961). While Desmond Pacey's essay in *Literary History of Canada* claims that this flourishing of Canadian magazines and journals "provided invaluable opportunities for young writers to try their wings," he does not by and large disclose the nature of the literary production.[13] If journals were ideologically predisposed to valorize some representations while discouraging others (witness the construction of the "aggressively masculinist and heterosexist" Canadian poetic canon,[14] for example), then their flourishing would have been of negligible benefit to an author submitting a *de trop* representation of sexuality.

How then, we might ask, might a publisher have responded to the manuscript nestled inside *Junior Homemaking*? Again, of course, we can only speculate. Considering that the novel graphically depicts (for the times) a sexual encounter between two men, its being published would have been putting on public display an act both criminal—and one not decriminalized until 1969—and distasteful. And because Winston's fateful sexual rendezvous would be arguably obscene, any interested publishing house would have understood its vulnerability to litigation. Furthermore, the very fact that the tradition of Canadian homosexual literature is

13. See "The Writer and His Public 1920-1960" in *Literary History of Canada*: 20.

14. See Dickinson's chapter, "Critical Homophobia and Canadian Canon-Formation" in *Here is Queer: Nationalisms, Sexualities, and the Literatures of Canada*, especially 69-78. Dickinson makes frequent reference to Robert K. Martin's essay, "Sex and Politics in Wartime Canada: The Attack on Patrick Anderson."

a scant one even today (we might recall, too, that what is arguably the first Canadian lesbian novel was set in Nevada and authored by the American-born Jane Rule in 1964)[15] suggests that to his own detriment the writer was ahead of his time. As another point of comparison, we might also pay attention to a question privately posed in 1960 by E.M. Forster—at the time one of England's most celebrated literary figures, the first president of the National Council for Civil Liberties, and the outspoken defender of the putative obscenity of Radclyffe Hall and D.H. Lawrence. On the cover page of his unpublished manuscript of *Maurice*, a novel begun in 1913 and "Dedicated to a Happier Year," he wrote: "Publishable—but worth it?" The question was answered in the affirmative only after *Maurice* appeared in 1971, one year after Forster's death.[16]

Canada was by no means exempt from the political acts of repression and tacit non-acknowledgement about which Forster elsewhere speaks. As the work of historians such as Tom Warner, Mary Louis Adams, and Gary Kinsmen have illustrated, the process of heterosexual normalization[17] was proceeding at full speed during the conservative post-War/

15. While scholars take note of both Sinclair Ross's *As For Me and My House* (1941) and Ernest Buckler's *The Mountain and the Valley* (1952) as novels that have "rich, though generally unacknowledged, homoerotic subtexts" (Tom Hasting "Gay and Lesbian Writing," *Encyclopedia of Literature in Canada*: 419), Scott Symons' *Combat Journal for Place d'Armes* (1967) is generally regarded as the first novel to represent gay sexuality as a having a full cultural complement. Tom Warner's history of queer activism in Canada, *Never Going Back*, anchors the appearance of the first openly lesbian and gay themes in film, theatre, visual art and literature in the early 1960s.

16. "Terminal Note" in *Maurice*: 240.

17. In *The Trouble with Normal*, Mary Louise Adams defines normalization as being an important aspect of moral regulation, "the social and political project of rendering 'natural' the perspectives and ideologies of hegemonic interests" (14).

Cold War period in Canada. Suffice it to say that the warning incorporated into a 1965 review of Rule's romantic debut novel—"*Desert of the Heart* is not recommended to those who find sexual perversion an uncomfortable subject"[18]—speaks volumes. In addition, the visible, active, and politically engaged community that is now taken for granted simply did not exist fifty years ago. Warner observes that Canada's first gay community organization did not form until 1964 (it was Vancouver's Association for Social Knowledge; the University of Toronto Homophile Association emerged some five years later). He notes, too, that overall perception of gays and lesbians after the Second World War was "profoundly negative" with few exceptions; even the "more liberal view held that homosexuality was morally wrong, deviant and disgusting,[19] but could be managed via psychoanalysis or medical treatment."[20] His overview is grim. And it is one that does not transform significantly until the emergence of gay liberation in the late 1960s. Warner concludes:

> For gays, lesbians, and bisexuals, Canadian laws, institutions, and social structures, historically, imposed a system of social oppression. Homosexuals generally were seen and treated as criminal, sinful, sick, degenerate, furtive—members of an undesirable, almost

18. A.C. Penta. *Best Sellers*. September 1, 1965: 222.

19. Compare E.M. Forster's "Terminal Note" in the typescript of *Maurice*: there's been a change in attitude in England, he observes, "from ignorance and terror to familiarity and contempt" (240).

20. *Never Going Back*: 43.

subhuman, group against which acts of bigotry, discrimination, injustice, and violence were tolerated or even encouraged.[21]

If the manuscript is an alluring puzzle of a historical document, its aspirations as literature are clear and warrant attention as well. If a credible author (or even authorial intent) cannot ultimately be fathomed to any degree, the literary design of the pages cannot be doubted: with its allusions, leitmotifs, and very structure, the manuscript is not coy about exhibiting its thoroughgoing knowledge of the novelistic tradition.

Consider just one example. On the first sheaf alone—featuring an excerpt (and new translation[22]) from Book II of Virgil's *Georgics*—we see that the author refers to Virgil's poetic examination of agriculture and then modifies the fragment to meet his own needs. The implicit comparison of urban and rural reverberating through Virgil's poem becomes an explicit one in the manuscript as the story's questing (Aeneas-like?) protagonist makes his three round trips

21. *Never Going Back*: 17. And codified in law and medical discourse. Warner notes that *Diagnostic and Statistical Manual of Mental Disorders*, first published in 1952, lists homosexuality as a sexual deviation—and can be located in the manual's "Sociopathic Personality Disturbances" section (24).

22. The unpublished translation poses its own questions. Is the translation the author's own or was he part of a social circle that included, for instance, a classics professor (or even a high school teacher at a tradition-minded private school) who not only provided a fresh take, but then gave it to the author for his novel's epigraph?

Then there is the question of the reference itself. While there is divided critical opinion of the intent of the ostensible farming manual of Publius Virgilius Maro (b. 70 B.C.), it is clear that the excerpt—related to the conservation of the strength of a farmer's flock that comes with isolating the afflicted animal—was chosen because it relates to the protagonist's dilemma. Avoiding love's "negative potential" (Putnam, Michael C.J. *Virgil's Poem of the Earth*: 199) and the chaos that emotion can bring to the social order, then, has obvious implications that reach far into the story of Winston Wilson.

to the city. Yet more than merely incorporating Virgil's conceit the author builds upon it, reshaping a classical model to meet his modern requirements. While *Georgics* utilizes the innate goodness that rural life fosters as a kind of role model for the poem's urban (Roman) audience, then *The Age of Cities* retains a steadfast ambivalence; in juxtaposing the two modes of living, the author proclaims that their relationship is not symbiotic. Rather, they are contiguous and discrete social systems, each one valuable in its own right and not subject to overlap. For Winston Wilson, the "values" of the two—the city is associated with darkness, the unknown, artifice and disguise, carnality, fraternity, insincerity, play, homosexuality, spontaneity (and one kind of truth), while the country is linked to daylight, fertility, nature, family, tradition, routine and familiarity, heterosexuality, abundance, repression (and another kind of truth)—have each their particular allure and utility. The unresolved duality of his character, in fact, comes to rely on both social systems.

Moreover, if the steady flow of references to classical authors—Ovid, Lucretius, Virgil—and poets of the modern period (Browning, Hardy, Eliot and so on) suggests[23] an author with a professional investment in literature or else an enthusiastic amateur (who, like Winston Wilson's touchstone Alexander Pope, has a fondness for the eternal

---

23. These speculations do not provide a satisfactory answer at all. It remains impossible to determine the author's social standing, level of education, or personal affiliations. For all one knows, the author might have been a Home Economics teacher with time on her hands, an avid appetite for literature and a burning desire to write a novel. It is tempting to believe that one of Canada's west coast modernists, Sheila Watson, filled those sheaves with her words. During WW II Watson taught high school in the most likely real-world counterpart to River Bend City, Mission, B.C. Unless she underwent to radical shift of themes and style, though, the manuscript could not have come from her hand.

symmetries of the classical poets), there is also the manuscript's correspondence to the vernacular and thematic developments of Canadian literature to consider. The author did not incorporate classical motifs and allusions in order to detach his story from a specific localized setting and then look fondly backwards to the surety of a Golden Age. He eschews the hermetic "soundproof, windowless, air-conditioned, and bombproof" place that MacGillivray envisions as the national novelists' favourite loitering spot, and sets the novel in specific geographical and socio-economic contexts. In truth, had the manuscript been published soon after it was finished, the novel (or its close attention to landscape and physical setting, in any case) would have found a secure placement in the critical work of Atwood (*Survival*) and Frye ("Conclusion," *Literary History of Canada*) that famously defined a fundamental Canadian literary property as an ambivalent relationship with the hostile land.

Placed in relation to other Canadian literature of the period, the manuscript exhibits thematic and stylistic commonalities with established figures, including Robertson Davies, Hugh MacLennan, and, in particular, Vancouver's Ethel Wilson. If the text itself positions the author as an adherent of a literary tradition that might look to W.H. Auden as its progenitor (in Canada, we might cite novelist David Watmough [b. 1926] and poet Daryl Hine [b. 1936] as Auden-inspired homosexual authors whose work fondly alludes to high cultural classical tradition), there is no overlooking that it shares qualities with the contemporaneous Canadian literature. The work is predominantly realist, according easily with Adele Wiseman's *The Sacrifice* (1956), Ethel Wilson's *The Swamp Angel* (1954) or Hugh MacLennan's *The Watch that Ends the Night* (1959). In its depiction of the small town we can see echoes of *Sunshine Sketches of a Small Town* (1912) as well as the critique of and pessimism about its narrowness as expressed, for instance, by Sinclair Ross' *As For Me and My House* (1941). It is Robertson Davies' *Salterton Trilogy* (1951-58), and its peculiar sincere affection for small town life (accompanied by a knowingness of its "cultural malnutrition" and the limitations which only a cosmopolitan city like London can remedy) to which a closer relationship might be considered at some future date. Though a questing narrator is a literary commonplace, Winston Wilson would keep good company equally with Maggie Lloyd of *The Swamp Angel* or any number of the beleaguered characters in the Salterton novels.

In hindsight, the decision to publish the manuscript came easily. Though there are sufficient aesthetic grounds to introduce the novel to contemporary readers, there are also broadly political ones. Whether a *roman à clef* or a conventionally Canadian realist account of social conditions circa 1959, the manuscript provides access to an invisible literary tradition and a virtually unknown subculture. One of the praiseworthy motivations of the pioneering essay collection *Hidden From History: Reclaiming the Gay and Lesbian Past* (1989) is (as its title states directly) making visible that which has been denied and hidden away. Publication of *The*

*Age of Cities*, then, supports that ongoing and pan-cultural enterprise.

In a sense, the manuscript lodged in *Junior Homemaking* performs a role often reserved for the conventional historical novel. As Helen Cam claims in her delightfully naïve 1965 pamphlet, the purpose of the "good" historical novel is to "fill in the lamentable hiatus of the historical record."[25] Guided by diligent research and a heightened "imaginative sympathy"[26] the historical novelist cautiously invents probable scenes and conversations—ones that the ethics-bound empiricist historian cannot—and so makes manifest that which has been presumed forever lost. Pondering *The Age of Cities* might also incite a recollection of Sigmund Freud's positivistic ease when confronted circa 1900 by the incomplete, indeed aborted, psychoanalysis of Ida Bauer. Publishing the sessions as "Fragment of An Analysis of a Case of Hysteria" (1905), Freud compares his efforts to those of "those discoverers whose good fortune it is to bring to the light of day after their long burial the priceless though mutilated relics of antiquity." While the surety expressed when he states "I have restored what is missing"[27] cannot be fully felt for the sheaves (and their still missing author) hoarded away in *Junior Homemaking*, it is our good fortune to have a chance to encounter a publication that prises a passageway open to an altogether obscure moment of the past.

25. *Historical Novels*: 7.

26. *The English Historical Novel*: 4.

27. "Fragment": 176.

A note on the typeface and the double "Epi":

One of the curious conditions of the manuscript was found in its concluding few pages. Labeled "Epi I Ap 65" and "Epi II Ap 65," the two bundles represent two similar but distinct epilogues. The absence of the author here is especially confounding because it prevents a determination of the true nature of this double ending (that recalls the early postmodern innovation of John Fowles' *The French Lieutenant's Woman* of 1969): was it designed as such, or did the author not have the time, ability, or inclination to complete the project by selecting one and discarding the other? As it stands, the suspended conclusion resounds provocatively.

The alternate endings are intriguing insofar as the two choices—resentment and subterfuge on the one hand and repression and willed "amnesia" on the other hand—in no way make a utopian projection into the future; in contrast to Forster's novel with its author's insistence upon a happy ending for his protagonist,[28] the anonymous author does not give the hero a like advantage. The author apparently could not reconcile the homosexual individual with traditional cultural formations. Cultural institutions and norms, in fact, while not oppressively phobic remain nonetheless rigidly heteronormative and unyielding to outside influences. The best that can be said is that an urban homosexual proto-culture (semi-visible at best: private residences, commercial establishments, a public park) exists and thrives in its marginal and miniscule niches.

Lastly, the manuscript featured a literary innovation

28. *Maurice*: vi.

that I have replicated in the present volume. Certain words or terms (such as "Malkin's" or "Errol Flung!") were differentiated from the handwriting, as though the author desired to imitate actual typography. Current typesetting technology with its myriad of fonts makes accommodation of this approach relatively simple.

— A.X.P. (Summer 2006)

# References

Adams, Mary Louise. *The Trouble With Normal: Postwar Youth and the Making of Heterosexuality*. Toronto: University of Toronto Press, 1997.

Cam, Helen. *Historical Novels*. London: Historical Association, 1961.

Davies, Robertson. *The Salterton Trilogy*. Toronto: Penguin, 1986.

Fleishman, Avrom. *The English Historical Novel: Walter Scott to Virginia Woolf*. Baltimore: Johns Hopkins Press, 1971.

Forster, E.M. *Maurice*. Toronto: Macmillan, 1971.

Foucault, Michel. "Nietzsche, Genealogy, History." *Language, Counter-Memory, Practice*. Ed. Donald F. Bouchard. Ithaca, NY: Cornell University Press, 1977: 139–164.

Freud, Sigmund. "Fragment of an Analysis of a Case of Hysteria." *The Freud Reader*. Ed. Peter Gay. New York: W.W. Norton, 1989: 172–238.

Kinsman, Gary. *The Regulation of Desire: Homo and Hetero Sexualities*. Montreal: Black Rose Books, 1996.

McPherson, Hugo. "Fiction (1940–1960)." *Literary History of Canada: Canadian Literature in English*. 2nd Ed. Ed. Carl F. Klinck. Toronto: University of Toronto Press, 1976: 205–233.

New, W.H. *A History of Canadian Literature*. London: Macmillan, 1989.

Pacey, Desmond. "The Writer and His Public (1920–1960)." *Literary History of Canada: Canadian Literature in English*. 2nd Ed. Ed. Carl F. Klinck. Toronto: University of Toronto Press, 1976: 3–21.

Penta, A.C. "Review of *Desert of the Heart*." *Best Sellers* 25. Sept 1, 1965: 222.

Putnam, Michael C.J. *Virgil's Poem of the Earth: Studies in the Georgics*. Princeton, N.J.: Princeton University Press, 1979.

Dickinson, Peter. *Here is Queer: Nationalisms, Sexualities, and the Literatures of Canada*. Toronto: University of Toronto Press, 1999.

Hastings, Tom. "Gay and Lesbian Writing." *Encyclopedia of Literature in Canada*. Ed. W.H. New. Toronto: University of Toronto Press, 2002: 418–422.

Warner, Tom. *Never Going Back: A History of Queer Activism in Canada*. Toronto: University of Toronto Press, 2002.